# PRAISE FOR *A DOLLAR'S WORTH*

I thoroughly enjoyed reading *A Dollar's Worth*. The complexity of the main character, the twists and turns of the plot, and the surprise ending kept my interest throughout.

June Husted, psychologist

*To Jerri & Bill;*
*what nice people you*
*are. We are so*
*happy we met you*
*in o- R.P.S.*
*God Bless You Both.*
*Jaug Chiseri*

# A DOLLAR'S WORTH

# A DOLLAR'S WORTH

## JOEY CHISESI & DIANE CHISESI

TATE PUBLISHING & *Enterprises*

Published by Tate Publishing & Enterprises, LLC
127 E. Trade Center Terrace | Mustang, Oklahoma 73064 USA
1.888.361.9473 | www.tatepublishing.com

Tate Publishing is committed to excellence in the publishing industry. The company reflects the philosophy established by the founders, based on Psalm 68:11,
*"The Lord gave the word and great was the company of those who published it."*

Book design copyright © 2010 by Tate Publishing, LLC. All rights reserved.
*Cover design by Kandi Evans*
*Interior design by Stefanie Rooney*

Published in the United States of America

ISBN:978-1-61663-548-0
1. Fiction, General
2. Fiction, Christian, General
10.05.13

# DEDICATION

From Joey Chisesi: To my wife, Cathie Chisesi, for her willingness to sit and watch her favorite movies on television all alone in our family room while I spent hours and hours in our den office authoring this novel. When I first met her in 1943, little did she know she'd become a writer's widow. Now that this novel is written, I can take her out to dinner.

# ACKNOWLEDGMENTS

From Joey Chisesi: Sincere thanks and appreciation go to my editor, tutor, and now a special friend, Sue Clark. She's one bright lady. Sue Clark wasn't afraid to become oh so darn critical. Thanks to a real pal, David Leventhal. Dave advised me to get some excitement into the novel's first few pages. Hey, Dave, did I do it?

# CHAPTER ONE

**W**ith the siren screeching and emergency lights reaching into the Las Vegas night, the ambulance threaded its way through traffic. Nate "The Wanderer" Bradford had collapsed following a turbulent battle in the ring at the Las Vegas arena. The brawl between Nate and Jimmy "Jumbo" Owens ended after Bradford scored a technical knockout over Owens, the rugged and more seasoned fighter.

In his dressing room after the bruising brawl, Nate's knees gave way, and he fell in the shower stall. Max "The Axe," a veteran in the fight business and Nate's trainer, grabbed a phone and dialed 911. "Send an ambulance, quick."

Max threw a robe around Nate and helped him to a dressing room table. He slapped Nate's face with both hands. "Come on, kid. Come on now. Say something. It's me, Max. Come on, kid. Pull it together."

Nate stared as Max cajoled him. In a couple minutes, two paramedics entered the dressing room pushing a litter.

The paramedics attached a blood pressure cuff to Nate's left arm and studied their monitor. One of them put a stethoscope to his chest. Nate began to feel a bit more alert.

"Okay, fella," Max said. "We're gonna take a ride to the hospital and have you gone over good. I don't think you're in serious trouble, but we gotta be sure."

Nate looked at an anxious Max.

"Las Vegas General," one paramedic said.

"Got it," came back Max's response. "I'll follow you best I can."

As the paramedics wheeled Nate outside the dressing room, Misty, his gal, rushed up to the litter. "Is he okay? Is he all right?"

"We think so, lady. We're headed for the emergency room."

"Come on," Max said, taking Misty's arm. "We'll follow the ambulance."

Nate sat on the edge of the emergency room bed. A worried-looking Max asked Nate if he knew his name.

"Yours or mine?" Nate tried to smile, but it hurt too much.

"Yours, kid. How about this pretty gal with worry all over her face? Who is she?"

"Come on, Max, are you a doctor now too?"

Misty touched Nate's hand and moved closer to him.

"Look, fella," Max said. "You won the fight tonight, but you took a heck of a poundin'. Now you know why I hesitated when you first asked to suit up and work out in my gym. Don't want you to get conceited, kid, but you know you're my special guy. I don't have the bruises on my face and forehead like you right now, but I hurt inside."

Misty reached for a tissue.

"I'm okay. Really."

"Oh, Nate, you think you're all right, but they're going to keep you here overnight just to be safe." Misty wiped her eyes.

"How about my agreeing?" Nate said. He found strength to raise his voice.

"Kid, they're concerned you got a mild concussion. You may feel okay, but we gotta play it safe. No matter how good you feel, you can't get back into the ring anyway, at least for sixty days."

That made Nate's heart jump a beat.

"That's the law. Not my rules. We gotta go by the law," Max said. "Just play it cool, kid. Relax. One night in the hospital won't kill ya."

Max grabbed Nate's other hand and patted it. "I have to secure the arena. You know the drill. Misty'll do just fine as your special nurse. Heck, if I had a choice, I'd switch with ya so she could take care of this ole guy." Max stepped closer to Misty and gave her a gentle kiss on her cheek.

Misty smiled. "Thank you, Max."

Max gave Nate the usual thumbs-up sign as he tugged on the curtain around the bed and disappeared.

Misty took Nate's left hand. "They don't think your hand's broken, Nate, but they're going to X-ray it just to be sure."

"Why? My hand's okay, Misty. I can move my fingers. I don't need an X-ray."

Just then, the curtain parted and a young emergency room physician came in accompanied by a nurse. "I'm Doctor Beltran. How're you doing, Mr. Bradford? Did your head hit the floor of the ring?

"I can answer that," Misty said. "I was there. His head didn't hit anything, but he was hit by the other guy a lot. Look at his forehead. Look at his eyes." Misty began to cry. "Nate, you've got to give up this boxing stuff. I can't bear to see you like this."

"That's something for you two to discuss, but for right now, I want you to tell me if you remember your head striking the floor of the ring," the doctor said. "I need to hear it from you."

Nate hesitated and then in a soft voice said, "I don't remember, Doc."

"Do you remember much about your fight?"

Nate covered his eyes with his hand. How could he answer the Doc when his head hurt so much and his ears buzzed so loud?

"What was the name of your opponent?"

Nate took a deep breath. "A black man. I'm not sure of his name right now."

Misty looked anxious. She asked if she could tell Nate.

The doctor nodded. "Let's see if you recognize his name, Nate."

"Jimmy Owens," Misty said. "That's his name." She grasped his hand a little tighter. "Do you remember now?"

"Yeah, sure. I knew it was something like that."

"I want to X-ray your right hand. An X-ray tech will be here shortly." Doctor Beltran gave the nurse some instructions and then left the room.

Nate closed his eyes as the nurse checked his blood pressure and took his pulse. He opened them in time to see her mark the results on a memo pad she'd taken from her pocket.

An X-ray technician entered Nate's room with a portable X-ray machine. "I'm Dave. I'm going to X-ray your right hand. Okay? There's nothing to this. Your doctor will have a look-see at the pictures right away. We'll know PDQ if your hand's broken."

Nate flexed his right hand. "I don't need that."

Misty said, "Please Nate. Please."

Nate grudgingly complied.

In a few minutes, the X-ray technician finished his task. "Thank you, Mr. Bradford." He left the room.

The nurse stood by. Then she said, "I'm going to put an IV needle in your arm and give you some medications. Doctor Beltran feels this will help you, Nate."

She turned took a needle from the cabinet and told Nate, "After what you've been through, this won't hurt a bit. Just relax your right arm." She left the blood pressure cuff on his left arm hooked up to a monitor.

Neither Nate nor Misty spoke until she finished inserting the needle. Then the nurse asked if Nate was comfortable sitting on the edge of the emergency room bed.

Comfortable? How could he be comfortable? Instead of trying to figure out what to say, Nate nodded yes. Then he looked at Misty. "I just want to get out of here."

"Nate, you've got to calm down, honey."

The doctor returned. He closed the curtain behind him and said, "From the pictures and the scan we took before, I don't see any major problems.

It's your responses and your vitals that we want to check some more. Your pulse rate is lower than normal for a chap your age. Your blood pressure is down a tad below where it should be also. Probably being an athlete accounts for that, but I'd like you to spend the night with us, Nate. We need to be on the safe side."

"See, honey?" Misty said. "Doc's right."

Nate let go of Misty's hand. This woman he cared for so much was beginning to irritate him. After all, he wasn't knocked stupid. He could still make up his own mind.

"I'll come back tomorrow and bring you home to my apartment. You be still. Relax. Okay?"

Doctor Beltran smiled at Nate. "Good. This young lady makes a lot of sense. It's settled then."

"No, it isn't."

"Come on, Nate. You'll be watched closer here," Doctor Beltran said. "By the way, that's a brutal game you're in, if anyone can call prizefighting a game."

Nate started to protest again, but Misty cut him off. "Nate will do it."

He wanted to swing his legs off the bed and take himself down the hall away from the Doc and his whimpering girlfriend. But just as he made the connection between his head and his legs, the nurse and the doctor left.

Misty grabbed Nate's hand again to rub it.

Why didn't she leave him alone? He wasn't a little kid. He was a boxer and a good one.

"You had Max and I very worried," Misty said.

Max and me, Nate corrected her in his head. See, he was just fine. He could still pick out a rare mistake in librarian Misty's grammar.

"Will Max be coming soon?" Nate could tell that his speech was still a little slurred.

"Oh, Nate, he was here. He left a little bit ago. Don't you remember?"

"Uh, oh, yeah. I think he kissed you on the cheek."

"You do remember." Misty then kissed Nate's cheek and managed to put her head on his shoulder. "You're okay. I knew it. But, Nate, you're going to have to give up boxing. That'll make me so happy."

Nate whispered, "I like boxing."

"You don't really mean that. Look where you are. God, Nate, you're in a hospital."

The nurse came back with a glass of water for Nate. "Could I bring you anything? How about a cup of coffee? We have decaf or a hot cup of tea maybe? Doctor said you may have something to drink if you wish."

Misty spoke. "A nice cup of tea would be fine for us with just a little sugar."

"No." Nate spoke as loud as he could. "I don't want tea."

"But, Nate, you always have tea with me."

The nurse returned with two tea bags, sugar, and some creamers.

Nate brushed her offer aside.

Misty thanked her. "He's just exhausted, really tired. He'll drink his tea later."

Misty sipped on her tea while Nate stared at her. She kissed him again and said, "Nate, I'll be here to pick you up tomorrow morning. Promise me you'll do what they tell you to do."

"Yeah. Okay. I'm not promising anything." He paused. "Oh, all right, Misty, I'll try."

• • •

When the night nurse came in with an ice bag, she placed it against his face. "My, goodness," she said. "You look like you've been in a bit of a fight. How's the other guy? I think I'd have to bet on him."

"And you'd have lost," Nate said. "You'd sure have lost."

"Boxing match?" the nurse said.

"Yeah. One heck of a fight all right."

"Well," the nurse said, "fight's over."

For the first time since he hit the floor in the ring, Nate tried to unwind. It was difficult. He kept thinking about his match with Owens. With his head clearing a bit more each minute, he began to think about his life.

# CHAPTER TWO

N ate remembered the night his father said he was leaving. "But you can't, Dad," Nate had said. His dad left anyway.

Nate longed for him to return. He looked forward to his dad's telephone calls, as did his younger sister, Terri Jo. They missed the fun times when his dad would take them for a ride in his motorboat.

Nate recalled the hours and hours his dad would be away from home. He was old enough then to realize the demands made on his dad's time, the requirement for being a detective on the Seattle police force. He knew too his mom had asked him many times to spend more hours at home even if it called for her husband to accept fewer assignments.

Their mother looked out for their education. "You've got to do your homework and study hard, both of you. An education's the only way to get ahead in this world. Your father wants to be proud of you, just like I do. Even though he's away from us, you know he loves you."

More than once, Nate heard his mother say to his father, "The kids need a father. You need to be home to help me with them."

His dad's answer was always the same. "Look, Priscilla, they're better off this way. They don't need to hear us bicker all the time. I'm not giving up my police work. I just can't throw that away." More than once Nate had heard his dad argue, "I have too many years on the force to just walk away from what I do."

Once, when Ted Jennings was at their home, Nate even overheard his dad's detective partner tell his father, "Johnny, your kids need you at home. I know you send money to Priscilla, but there's more to being a father than just that. Good Lord, look at the cases we deal with. Most all these bad situations stem from separations. And they're just too common now days. You know what I'm talking about."

If there was any good thing about his folk's domestic problem, it was Nate's mom being a stay-at-home mom. She was always there when the kids came home from school. And Johnny never failed to send support money to Priscilla, always on time.

She was an excellent seamstress. Neighbors brought their clothes to her for alterations. With the extra money Priscilla earned, she'd take the kids out for pizza or to McDonald's, sometimes to see a movie.

Nate never heard his mom discuss marital problems in front of him or Terri Jo. She never put Johnny down in their presence. After all, Johnny was their father. His mom even told him and his sister how much she loved their dad.

Then, on a rather typical, dreary Sunday in Seattle, Nate's dad made an appearance at their home, along with Ted. Jennings was Nate's godfather, but Nate and Terri Jo called him Uncle Ted. Jennings had been to their home many times over the years, usually to pick up Nate's dad or bring him home.

As he relaxed in the hospital, Nate remembered one particular Sunday afternoon when Uncle Ted came to babysit. Twelve-year-old Nate and Terri Jo, who was eight then, were going to watch a Seattle Seahawk football game on TV with him.

To Nate's surprise, his mom and dad were going out for a boat ride, something his dad enjoyed. The day turned dreary, not one that would be very enjoyable for boat rides on the Puget Sound waters between Seattle and Tacoma.

Nate knew his dad was a skilled boatman,

so a misty day in Seattle was anything but a rare happening.

Nate was a well-coordinated young man. Before the game started, Nate and Uncle Ted threw a football around. Terri Jo joined in, although at her age she wasn't nearly as coordinated as Nate. Terri Jo could draw. That was something Nate couldn't do.

As game time for the Seahawks arrived, Jennings and Nate returned to the house. Passing a hallway mirror, Terri Jo posed in front of it. Jennings said, "My, you're going to be a gorgeous chick some day. You've got eyes I bet a lot of other gals wished they had. Mark my words, young lady in the mirror."

Nate cut in front of her and laughed. "What about this football player, Uncle Ted? Look at these muscles."

Jennings grinned. "You both'll wind up being models."

"No, I want to be an artist," Terri Jo said.

Nate tugged at her hair that hung down to her shoulders. "I'll be your protector. I'll make sure no one teases you. You watch. I'm going to be as tall as Dad, maybe taller. How tall are you, Uncle Ted?"

"Six foot two. Your dad's as tall as I am."

"I guess there's no way I'll have red hair like you. Mine's dark."

"I'll bet the girls are already looking you over, Nate. How tall are you now?"

"I'm almost five feet seven inches, and it's all cold steel."

"Cold steel? Where did you pick that phrase up? Well, between you both, you make a great brother and sister team."

Nate helped his mother and father hitch the boat trailer to the rear of his dad's minivan. They waved good-bye to Terri Jo and Nate after plunking kisses on their cheeks. Johnny gave a thumbs-up sign to Jennings. *A good omen,* Nate remembered thinking, *for his folks to be in such a happy mood.*

After the Seattle Seahawk football game was over, about five, Jennings said, "Your folks should be home pretty quick."

Soon, six o'clock rolled around and then seven and eight. Darkness descended on the city. Lights went on in the neighborhood.

The three of them had finished microwaved chicken pot pies when Jennings said, "Let's hope those two love birds are talking about your dad's coming home to roost again. Wouldn't that be something?"

The suggestion that his dad would come back home to live was almost more than Nate could wish for. Then Nate saw his uncle Ted use his cell phone to call precinct headquarters. He heard the words. "Nothing unusual, right? Okay, Sarge. If you happen to get anything, call me."

Jennings's anxiety began to show. He told Nate

his father was in the habit of checking in with their precinct. Why he hadn't checked in was a puzzle.

By now, nine o'clock had come around, and Jennings and Nate had tucked Terri Jo in bed. Jennings dialed the police station again. This time he spoke to the duty sergeant, demanding an answer. Why didn't anyone know the whereabouts of Johnny Bradford and his wife, Priscilla?

When he hung up, Jennings made another call, this time to the coast guard. Nate now had a queasy feeling in his stomach. Jennings explained the situation to a coast guard official. Then he said, "No rough seas reported? No distress calls? Just poor visibility, huh?"

Nate's stomach settled down a little. With reluctance, Nate put on his pajamas and went to bed. Jennings said he'd stretch out on the couch to wait for Nate's folks to return.

• • •

At midnight, with no sign of the Bradfords' return, Jennings mumbled to himself, "This isn't like Johnny. What the devil could have happened?"

He phoned precinct quarters. The duty sergeant told him, "Relax, Jennings, they probably went off to a motel to be alone. They're okay. Johnny's a big boy."

"I don't care how big Johnny is; something's

going on. Hey, this guy's my partner. Know what that means?"

"Yeah, I do. I'll tell you again. Johnny's a big boy. He can take care of himself and his wife. Relax. Cool it."

Jennings looked for coffee in the cupboard. Trying to understand the situation better, he called the coast guard station at Shilshole Bay in Puget Sound. The petty officer manning the phone said, "Look, we've had no distress calls, no problems. A misty day like we had usually means less action out there. I got your message when I took duty tonight. I'll call if anything turns up."

Jennings's stomach churned. He had the awful feeling that detectives get when they know something isn't kosher, not going right. He tried to sleep, but it was almost impossible. His mind was focused on the worst scenario.

In the early morning, Nate awoke to find Jennings in the kitchen. "Did Mom and Dad come home?" he said. Maybe he slept through the commotion they would have made.

"No, son. They probably spent the night together. You know, just to be together."

Nate left the kitchen, went upstairs, and tickled Terri Jo into getting up, at the same time trying to pretend everything was okay. Both Nate and Terri Jo got ready for school.

Before Jennings took the kids to school, he said,

"Nate, do you have a key to the garage? Just want to take a quick peek."

Nate tagged along with Jennings. "Obviously the boat wouldn't be in there," Jennings told Nate. But when he stepped inside the garage, he said, "Oh, my God, Nate. They drove off yesterday without their life jackets."

Nate counted them. Four life jackets hung on the garage wall; two were adults and the other jackets were his and Terri Jo's.

"Darn it, Nate," Jennings said. "Was your dad so wrapped up with their get-together that he forgot the life jackets?"

# CHAPTER THREE

J ennings saw to it that Nate and Terri Jo had lunch provisions and then herded them into his car and headed off to their school. He dropped them in front of the school building, watched them enter, and then did a U-turn to work his way into the school parking lot. Not bothering to lock his doors, Jennings hastened to find the school office where he asked to see someone in charge. He showed his police detective's badge and was led to a school counselor's office.

"I'm detective Ted Jennings," he said, a bit nervous. "I've been watching, I mean taking care of the Bradford children, Nate and his little sister, Terri Jo."

Mrs. Riddle said, "Oh, yes. I'm the school counselor."

"I have a terrible worry and sinking feeling."

"In what way? Are the children all right?"

"Oh, yes, they're okay. They're right in class where they belong. You probably haven't seen them yet, but it's their parents I'm concerned about."

"What?" Mrs. Riddle said.

Ted explained how the Bradfords went for a boat ride and then, in the middle of his explanation, he said, "You do know they've been living apart, don't you?"

"Yes, yes. We're aware of it. We try to be especially protective of the children here at Cleveland. You know we live in a world of single parenthood. Children are more at risk because of this, and ..." she stopped. "Oh, I'm sorry. What's the problem?"

"The Bradfords never came home last night, and they didn't come home this morning, at least up to when I left for school with the kids. This isn't my partner's MO. I mean, this isn't the way Johnny, uh, Mr. Bradford does things. We've been a team in the detective unit for some time, and Johnny was in the navy. But, come of think of it, he was always on shore patrol, you know, a military policeman. I'm getting rattled now. I'm really, really worried."

"Oh, dear God," Mrs. Riddle muttered. "Do the children know?"

"Nate has a pretty darn good idea," Jennings

said, "And little Terri Jo, well, I think she may know something's going on."

"How can you find out about their parents? You're a detective, aren't you?" She paused. "Oh, I'm sorry. I didn't mean that the way it sounded. You know what I mean. Can't the police find them?"

Just then, Mrs. Riddle's phone rang.

"Excuse me, Detective." She answered the phone. "Oh, yes. He's right here. Detective, it's for you." She handed him her phone.

Jennings said, "I'll be there in about fifteen minutes."

"Was that call about the Bradfords?"

"Yes, yes. It doesn't sound good," Jennings answered. The coast guard found the remains of a boat about two miles off shore. One of the larger pieces has the letters JOH and another piece has NNY O. That's the name of the craft. *Johnny O.* Oh, God!"

"What do you want the school to do?"

"Right now, nothing till I learn more. It looks bad, real bad. The guard found no signs of life in the shattered remains of the boat or in the water. Looks like they were run into by another boat and whoever was piloting that craft didn't report a thing. Please just make sure the kids are okay. I'm not ready to tell them anything at this point."

Jennings asked for the phone number of the school and for her extension. "I'm going to the coast guard building, and I'll be in touch with you as the day progresses."

Mrs. Riddle reached her hand out as if in consolation.

"If it means keeping them a while after school, we'll do that. I'll wait to hear from you."

Jennings shook her hand with both of his. "I'll see to it that someone cares for them. Don't release the kids to anyone unless I give you the authority."

"We wouldn't anyway."

"Oh, yeah. I'll identify myself to you by phone, or have whoever comes to get them use a code word. Let's see, something regarding their boat. Let's see, yeah, let's go with *Johnny O*. Yeah."

Jennings thanked her and headed out of her office. When he reached his car, Jennings stuck his arm out the window, put his red flashing light on the roof, and began a fast trip to the coast guard building. As he drove, he turned his dispatch radio on and reached his precinct headquarters.

"This is Detective Ted Jennings. I won't be in my office for a while. Tell the watch sergeant I'm checking on what seems to be a boat wreck. Detective Bradford and his wife, Priscilla. I'm afraid things are bad, real bad."

The speaker squawked, "Oh no. No, Jennings, not Johnny?"

"Yep," Jennings said. "But we're not totally sure."

Then Jennings called the dispatcher back. "This

is Detective Jennings. Look, I need the U.S. Coast Guard phone number. Skip that request. Patch me through to the coast guard station."

"I can handle that."

Jennings asked the duty officer at the Shilshole Coast Guard Station, "Just exactly where can I get a boat so I can see the *Johnny O* wreckage?"

"Come to our dock. We'll have a craft ready for you. Would you like to talk with the station commander?"

Jennings continued to drive down Seattle's streets as a calm voice said, "Detective Jennings, this is Commander Wittgren. Has this matter been assigned to other officers as yet?"

Jennings said his precinct had put out a bulletin alerting detectives and patrolmen to watch out for any boats showing signs of damage to the hull, particularly the bow of any craft with white stains on it.

"We're searching likewise," Wittgren said. "We're holding to the information we received earlier. Looks like another craft rammed them broadside on the port side. We've received calls at the station reporting a collision so we have to conclude it was a hit and run. Do you know who was piloting the victim's craft?"

"I'm 99 percent positive it was my partner, Johnny Bradford, and his wife, Priscilla. Johnny's my partner. God, I may have to say was my partner."

"Sorry, Detective."

"Jennings, Detective Ted Jennings."

"Jennings, I'm really sorry. They apparently didn't have life jackets on."

"I know. I know. I found four jackets in their garage. Two were kids' and the other two were for the Bradfords. They were trying to patch up their marriage. Johnny must have spaced out about the jackets somehow. It just wasn't like him to do that."

Wittgren cut in. "Are you sure he accidentally forgot them?"

"What's that supposed to mean? Johnny was my partner. He was a good—is a—good cop. You're not suggesting ... "

"Sorry, Jennings. But you mentioned patching up a marriage."

"That's what I meant, reconciling. They loved each other. Forget that stuff, Wittgren. Just drop it."

"Okay, Jennings. It's my job, as you know. I have to be a sea detective just like you're a detective on shore."

Jennings, a couple minutes away, said, "Thanks. Then he muttered, "How could that guy think it was anything but an accident?"

# CHAPTER FOUR

Jennings managed to worm his way into the coast guard grounds where he was met by two coast guardsmen. "I'm Detective Ted Jennings. Any of my men show up yet?"

"Yes, sir," replied one of the two sailors. "Two guys are down by the launching pier waiting for you."

"Good," Jennings said. "Let's have at it."

Jennings followed the two coast guardsmen to the end of the pier and climbed down to a coast guard craft. Detectives Carron and Forrestor were already aboard. In a few minutes, the small boat headed out to the bay.

"How far is it?" Jennings said.

"About two miles, sir. We have a salvage craft

out there marking the exact spot where we found the parts. We should be there in about fifteen minutes, sir."

"Well," Jennings said, looking at Mike Carron and Jack Forrestor, "Cat got your tongues?

"No, Ted," Forrestor said, "It's just that, well, you know, this isn't just any old case. This is our family. What the heck can we say? If what we think happened, some rotten creeps are loose in this area. This is like a hit and run case. They're sure guilty of manslaughter."

"You look terrible, Ted, like you've been up all night," Carron said.

"Well, I didn't exactly have what you call a comfortable night's sleep."

The three of them sat in silence for a few minutes, and then Carron said, "Great Seahawk game yesterday. Do you think it was a good idea to put the Hawks in the other league?"

"How can you talk about football at a time like this, Carron?" Forrestor said.

"I can't blame you for trying to get our minds off this nightmare," Jennings said. "All I can think of right now are those two Bradford kids."

"Do they know?" Forrestor said.

"I think the boy has a good idea. He's twelve. He's the oldest. The little girl's only in the fourth grade. She's probably unaware of this mess. I told the counselor at their school about the situation.

God, I have to tell Johnny and Priscilla's folks when I get back to the station."

"What a mess," Forrestor added. "What a rotten mess."

One of the young sailors spoke up. "It's probably a good idea, fellas, to keep our eyes open for anything floating in the water. Don't mean to tell you guys what to do, of course."

Everyone looked in the direction of the salvage boat a few hundred yards away.

Forrestor said, "No bodies found, huh?"

The other coast guardsman said, "Negative, sir. No life jackets either."

Jennings said, "Then you've already been out here?"

"No, sir. I overheard the duty officer talking on the ship to shore radio. He acted puzzled because no jackets were found, sir."

"Well, it's no secret, at least it won't be for very long," Jennings said. "Unless Johnny had life jackets stowed aboard the boat somewhere. I found four of them hangin' in the garage. Two of them were kids and the other two adults."

"Thank you, sir," one of the sailors said. "Looks like we're here."

As the smaller craft pulled alongside the salvage vessel, one of the crewmen shouted, "Pull 'er close, Sailor. Closer now!"

The crewman dropped a rope ladder. He dropped another rope to secure the boat to the larger vessel.

All three detectives managed to climb aboard. Once on deck, the mate in charge said, "Follow me. You can examine what we've been able to pull aboard so far."

A terrible quiet came over everyone as the detectives walked aft. There they saw large segments of a boat, white in color with edges that looked like they'd been whipsawed. One piece had JOH painted on it, and another had some letters so faint they were hard to read. But Ted knew they were NNY O.

"God. Oh, God almighty," Jennings said. "No mistaking this. That's the *Johnny O.*"

Detective Carron slammed his fist against the largest piece of wreckage. "Those creeps will pay for this. They'll pay."

The skipper of the salvage ship said, "That's a positive identification then?"

"Yes. It's Johnny's boat," Jennings said.

"What about the engine?" Forrestor said. "Where's the motor and, what do ya call it, the propeller?"

"The motor's at the bottom the bay. We haven't had a chance to look for it. Doesn't appear that would be important in this case though. This mess was caused by another craft, obviously plowed right smack into your friend's boat. They didn't exactly leave a note or a business card either or stop to apologize or look for survivors."

"Look," Jennings said, trying to hide his emotions. "What are the chances they survived and were picked up by another ship or boat? You know what I mean?"

"No chance, I'm afraid. I'd say your friends drowned or were hurt so severely at impact they didn't have a prayer. Davey Jones's locker's got two more." The skipper pointed downward to the bay waters.

"Can we learn anything from diving for the engine?" Forrestor asked.

"Afraid not," the skipper said. "We may find collision damage to it, but these big hunks pretty much tell the story. A pretty lousy way of doing things, I would say."

"Yeah, how about adding cowards or killers? That's what the crumbs are, lousy killers."

"Well, there's more," the skipper said. "See those empty beer cans over there and these empty bottles? We found them floating right by the wreckage."

"Jeez," said Carron, "I thought maybe those were your guys'."

"Hey, Detective, give me a break. If there's one thing that's forbidden, it's alcohol aboard a coast guard vessel. I'm going to assume that the guys who smacked into your friend's craft were drunk. I'd say they'd been drinking all day. I'd be willing to testify that this tragedy was alcohol induced. Then add to it the sloppy weather. I don't think your friends ever had a chance."

Forrestor said, "Yeah, and look at the beer cans. They're Bud cans. Johnny only drank Millers, and he wouldn't be drinking out here anyway."

Carron had a notepad and was jotting down notes as the skipper spoke. He looked at the skipper and said, "We get bodies washed ashore from time to time, and we're able to identify most of them. Will the Bradford bodies surface here or be washed ashore?"

Jennings seemed to close his eyes at Carron's question. "Carron."

"Sorry, Ted, but we've got to face the facts. No reports of rescues out here. No trace of the Bradfords and nothing but trashed pieces of their boat. What do you expect, Ted?"

"I know. I know," Jennings said. "I just don't want to admit this happened. I guess I'm in denial."

"Facts are facts," Forrestor said. "Evidence is evidence. All that's missing are the bodies."

"That's what hope is all about. We don't have Johnny or Priscilla." Jennings couldn't help but look out at the bay.

The skipper said, "One of you asked the question about where we might find their bodies. That's a bit of a tough question. They may wash ashore from the flow of the currents, or they may bloat and

JOEY CHISESI AND DIANE CHISESI

float. Sorry." He paused. "They might surface and be spotted by someone, but I wouldn't bet on either one. It's also possible one of them may be tangled with the steering cable or the prop. We just don't know yet."

Carron said, "Can you dive for them? This can't be too deep out here. There must be a way to spot them."

"That's not my department. Commander Wittgren hands out those orders. But you're detectives, and if you suspect foul play—and this looks like you could classify this mess as an incident of foul play—you guys can order divers to search for them, can't you?"

"This certainly doesn't come under the classification of a planned homicide. This is manslaughter," Jennings said.

"Well, that's the best we can offer at this time, Detective. I'm 90 percent certain a couple drunks, maybe more, smacked into this boat. The boat was battered, and the occupants were either seriously injured or in shock. When they got knocked overboard, they drowned. And, I add again, if we recover their bodies, we may find the answer to those two possibilities."

"Well, men," Forrestor put in, "let's meet with the commander, coast guard commander that is. We'll call our captain and fill him in on what we know."

"And I've got to make that phone call to the Bradford kids' school and find Johnny and Priscilla's relatives."

The coast guardsmen revved up the dinghy's motor and, almost in respect for the missing Bradford couple, circled the search site once before taking Jennings, Forrestor, and Carron back to shore.

# CHAPTER FIVE

J ennings told Carron and Forrestor it might be a good idea to check out paint stores and see if any purchases were made that might connect the hit-and-run culprits with the probable death of the Bradfords.

"You bet. That's just what we were gonna do," Forrestor said. "We'll update Captain Custer about what we saw and what we believe, urge him to delay a media announcement too. The kids may learn about this before you get to tell them. News now might scare our suspects out of town."

"Okay, guys. Thanks. Good luck."

"You too, Ted. Hope the visit with the kids goes well, but I can't imagine it will," Carron said.

The small craft pulled alongside a pier. Jennings asked one of the guardsmen, "Can you take me to Commander Wittgren?"

"Yes, sir," came the prompt reply. "He's waiting on you now."

Jenning's escort left him with Wittgren and departed. "Looks like you've gotten all the sad details as we know them. I'm sorry. I know they were your friends."

"*Were* seems the right word now, Commander. I don't think my miracle is happening."

"One of you asked about divers. We can arrange for a team if that's what you want. All I need is a request in writing. Even a phone call from your captain will do."

Jennings thanked him. With that settled, he began to leave. But Wittgren caught him off guard when he said, "By the way, have you found the Bradfords' vehicle? There might be a clue to some of this in there. Know what I mean?"

"Dog gone it, I'm the detective, and I forgot all about that."

"Yeah, check all the boat ramps and piers where Bradford might have parked."

"Can I use your phone? Oh, never mind," Jennings said. "I'll use my own car radio."

He called headquarters and told the desk sergeant he needed a search for the Bradford's van.

"We're already on that, Jennings."

"Oh, good. That's it for now."

Wittgren put out his right hand. "Well, Detective, our thoughts are with you. We take things like this as seriously as you do."

Jennings found the school counselor's card and dialed Mrs. Riddle. "This is Detective Jennings, code word Johnny O."

"What have you learned, Detective?"

Jennings didn't go into all the details, but he did inform her there was no indication that either his partner or his wife survived.

"Oh, how terrible. Oh, those poor children."

Jennings asked if there were professional counselors who dealt with situations like this. Mrs. Riddle told him yes and added she was one herself. Riddle stated that when many emergencies occur to families throughout the country with kids in schools, professionals, in addition to her, were on call for just such situations.

He suggested she call for added help. Jennings advised her he was going to the Bradford home to find Priscilla's address book in order to call both grandparents.

He told her he'd be back at the school at three. "I need to be there when we tell the kids the bad news." He asked if she could have the other counselors available then.

Riddle promised to do her best. "I'll get right

on it." She added, "I won't do anything with the children till you get here."

Jennings told Riddle they'd still use the code word until things were under control, hoping this would avoid leaking things to the children until at least three. He asked her not to discuss anything with anyone other than the school principal.

Jennings headed his unmarked car toward the Bradford home a few miles away from the coast guard station. Knowing that urgency would best serve his need, he put his red flasher on top of the car and picked up speed.

As he pulled into the Bradford driveway, one of the Bradford neighbors approached him. "Something wrong, Officer?"

"I'm Johnny's partner on the police force. Who are you?"

"Larry. I live next door. My wife and I keep an eye out for Mrs. Bradford and the kids. We know her husband is a detective, but he's not around very much. I guess you already know that."

"Look, I can't say very much at this time about the Bradfords, but could you do me a favor and keep your eye on the house?"

"Sure. Just tell me, are the children okay? Can I ask that?"

"Yeah, sure. They're fine. I may need your help later this afternoon. What's your phone number?"

Larry obliged.

Using the key he'd taken that morning, Jennings entered the Bradfords' house. He headed for Priscilla's bedroom and began to search the dresser, hoping to find an address book that would give him the phone numbers of Johnny's parents in Chicago or Priscilla's father in Wilmington, North Carolina.

Not finding what he was looking for, Jennings went into the kitchen. He saw a magazine on the kitchen counter; he looked under it and found a slim, brown address book. Thumbing through it, he searched for the grandparents' names.

Jennings put one hand on the Bradford's phone and gathered his thoughts. "Wait a minute," he said aloud. "I gotta call the police station in their town. I can't drop this bomb on people without someone being there with them." He dialed assistance from an operator. "This is Seattle, Washington, Police Detective Ted Jennings. I need the Park Ridge, Illinois, Police Department Headquarters."

He dialed the number. A desk clerk responded. Jennings explained what he wanted as clear as he could, considering how nervous he was. He wrote it down on a pad of paper next to the phone.

Then he searched for the phone number of Priscilla Bradford's father in North Carolina.

# CHAPTER SIX

**T**erri Jo woke from a troubled sleep. After grabbing her favorite stuffed animal, she tiptoed to her brother's bed and nudged him awake. The moonlight dribbled through the window of their room and onto his bed.

In the quiet darkness, she and Nate talked about the reality of their parents not returning. They spoke in whispers, trying to reassure the other that they would always be there for each other. Terri Jo snuggled on Nate's shoulder, watching the moonlight flicker across the window until she fell asleep.

• • •

The next morning, Jennings sat in the Riddles' kitchen. Mrs. Riddle had agreed to keep Nate and Terri Jo for the next few days. He and Mrs. Riddle needed to plan a memorial service, and they still had not found the grandparents.

Terri Jo and Nate had slept until eight. "We're late for school," Nate said as he and Terri Jo came into Mrs. Riddle's kitchen.

"I think you two should take a day off. What do you think about that?" Mrs. Riddle smiled. "And I'll stay home with you."

"Okay," Terri Jo said. She gave Mrs. Riddle a hug.

Nate frowned. "How come?"

Both Jennings and Mrs. Riddle explained the circumstances and what had to be done. He continued to frown; Jennings noticed tears rolling down Nate's cheek. The poor kid was beginning to realize what lay ahead for him and his sister. Jennings wished he could save the kids from their heartache.

"After you've freshened up, Uncle Ted will take you out for breakfast. Sound okay for you two?" Mrs. Riddle's voice cracked as she spoke.

"We'll all go together," Jennings said. "How about your husband, Mrs. Riddle? Would he like to join us?"

"Oh, I'm sure he would. He loves Denny's breakfasts."

Just then, a news bulletin on the radio interrupted their conversation. Police were on the scene at the Shilshole Coast Guard Station where detectives were inspecting the damaged sections of a small motor craft in an attempt to find clues to the disappearance of Seattle Police Detective Johnny Bradford and his wife.

Coast Guard Commander Wittgren made a statement concerning the tragedy and the coast guard's willingness to assist with the investigation.

Mrs. Riddle put her arms around Nate and Terri Jo as the four of them listened to the rest of the report.

Then Jennings said, "Well, gang, let's go and grab something to eat. Ready now?"

Mrs. Riddle removed a card from her wallet, picked up the telephone, and dialed social services. She was placed on hold, a familiar pattern when dealing with that agency. After a wait of some five minutes or so, a case worker she knew came on the line. Riddle told her about the Bradford incident, the tenuous situation with the grandparents, and her willingness to keep the children with her, at least for the time being. She also explained she was working with a Detective Ted Jennings, all of this to ensure compliance with King County rules.

The social worker agreed to the two youngsters staying with Mrs. Riddle for the present time.

Before leaving the Riddle residence, Jennings said to Nate and Terri Jo, "I've got to get to work now. You'll be fine with Mr. and Mrs. Riddle. They'll keep you busy for the next few days."

After another day and a number of phone calls, Jennings and Mrs. Riddle found the grandparents. They all decided that until the grandparents arrived in Seattle, final decisions should be postponed like the memorial service and what should happen to the kids. Jennings could tell that the elder folks were not in the greatest emotional shape by any means, probably not in the best physical condition either.

# CHAPTER SEVEN

Two days later, Jennings met the senior Bradfords, along with Christopher St. Lawrence, Priscilla's father, at Seattle's SEATAC Airport. He had made hotel reservations for them, and so the next day they all met in the lobby of Hotel Seattle to make plans for the memorial service. Of course, the subject of the Bradford children's custody came to the surface with no evidence or indication that any of the grandparents were willing to move to the northwest or assume custody of the children.

Jennings couldn't understand this at first, but as they spoke of their ages and infirmities, he began to realize they could be grandparents but in no way custodians. His heart sank.

For Jennings, the memorial services served to further depress him. As one of the speakers at the service, he found it hard to finish his eulogy. Jennings remained depressed for days. The senior Bradfords and Mr. St. Lawrence also appeared depressed, devastated with their losses.

Jennings received orders to meet with the police psychologist. Captain Casper, his boss, suggested he take a month's leave. Jennings declined. He figured the only way to get beyond his depression was to bury himself in work. Trish Murdock became his new partner, and a semblance of normality slowly entered his life.

Jennings, some fifteen years older than Murdock, took on the responsibility of teaching her some tricks of the trade, lessons above and beyond her police school training. They both became bent on finding the perpetrators of the dastardly ocean deed.

At the same time, life for the Bradford kids took on the form of a shuffle. Nate and Terri Jo were left to the dictates of the foster parent program. Although Jennings kept in touch with the kids as best he could, he could feel the distance growing between them and him.

# CHAPTER EIGHT

Nate grew from a wiry youngster to a strong, well-built teenager. He and Terri Jo's contact with Jennings became even less frequent. To Nate's distress, he lost contact with Terri Jo also.

Many times, Nate had become belligerent due to his problems with a number of his foster families. He'd say, "No. You can't make me do that" to a foster father. Or, "No. I don't care what you say. I'm not going to do that." Bitterness and frustration replaced the sensitivity he had as a younger boy.

On several occasions, Nate ran away from his foster care parents. He'd actually warn them before he did. "I'm not coming home after school." But he'd be caught by juvenile authorities and returned to a home, much to the discomfort of all. He was close to being a young inmate in a juvenile detention home.

Finally, after he received his high school diploma, Nate got into an argument with a foster dad. The foster dad said to him, "Nate, you've been drinking, haven't you?"

Nate shot back, "So what? Everybody does it."

His foster dad said, "I don't care what the other kids do. You're living in my house. You'll do what I tell you. You don't drink and live here. Understand?"

"I don't want to live here anyway with you or your rules."

It turned into a bad shouting match. His foster dad told him to go to his room and stay there. "You're grounded. Do you hear me? Go to your room." And in frustration he yelled, "Get out of my sight."

The next day, Nate packed his bags and left without a word. He fled from Seattle, hitchhiking one car after another, usually with a bottle in his hand. Nate jumped on to trains where he met with other transients, although he hadn't quite hit that low a level as yet.

One night, Nate headed for a nearby road and started to hitchhike through Oregon. He ended up by a lumber mill near a railroad track in Eureka, California. There, he picked up a job in a restaurant and sent himself to a small junior college. He finished one quarter at Eureka Junior College.

Nate lived from hand to mouth. At the school, he managed to acquire a few friends. He'd tell them how much he missed his parents and his sister. But he continued drinking, which only brought out more of his bitterness. Drinking cost him his job. He jumped on a freight train and found his way to Nevada.

Nate sat in a park in Carson City, hoping to avoid the cops who routinely patrolled the area. He, along with other loners, slept in fields and disappeared in the morning hours. Freight trains passed at frequent intervals, sounding their shrill horns to warn motorists and pedestrians. Depending on his mood, he'd stick around the area or hit the rails to another town. Nate had no idea where he was headed.

One morning, lying on newspapers, Nate pushed aside a few leaves off his legs. He found an empty bottle by his side, raised it to eye level, and then threw it down. He'd finished off the bottle the night before.

The rumble of a nearby train subsided and the earth felt still once more. Nate rubbed his eyes and, scratching his back, stood up.

His mood was changing again, agitated and without booze. During the night, he had been aware of a few guys lying around in the nearby grass. He'd butted heads once or twice with them since riding the rails and, on this particular morning, was in no mood for their wisecracks or game playing. He needed to get back on the rails and move on. But first, Nate sought a pub or store, anyplace where he could steal some booze.

Railroad tracks ran through the middle of many towns, most often parallel to a major highway or road. Walking to stores where booze was sold never was a problem for Nate and all the other hobos riding the rails.

Nate was always surprised when he arrived in a new town. For the most part, he never remembered what he did after jumping a train. He usually carried a bottle and drank until darkness. Then he would jump out of the boxcar and the whole episode would repeat itself.

Trains were nothing to fool around with. Their enormous size was overwhelming, but there were other worries along the routes, like train jumpers and the authorities. Train jumpers were a dying breed, and only a select group could endure this kind of life. Nate was among those tough, select guys.

From the corner of his eye he saw a small convenience store with a telephone booth. He felt confident the booth held a telephone book with all the information he needed about the town he was in. "Good," he mumbled to himself. It looked as if a phonebook was hanging by a chain. Nate picked up his pace.

Once he reached the store, he walked toward the booth and slung the phonebook up into his hands and then placed it on the metal shelf. By the size of the phonebook, he could tell the town wasn't very big. He moistened his fingers and flipped through the pages. Most phonebooks offered a map of the area. He located his position in relation to the railroad tracks.

Nate looked up liquor stores and any other kind that would carry liquor of any sort. He found the address of a small shopping area a few blocks over that had a bottle shop. He memorized the location of another. As he walked away from the telephone booth, he was disturbed over his dirty-looking appearance. "I need to wash my face. I'm a mess. I don't want to stand out looking like I do." He found a Burger King and used the restroom.

With the Burger King behind him, Nate picked up his pace. He'd have to steal the booze because he was short of money. He decided he'd rather drink than eat, so he continued to focus on the task at hand.

Hunger and booze had a way of making Nate do many things he wouldn't have done if life had been different. But Nate had become derailed after his parents' death and his separation from Terri Jo. Going from one foster home to another hadn't helped either. They fought with his mind.

Nate saw a grocery store as he walked up the sandy, chipped sidewalk toward a shopping complex. Across from the buildings was a park, and as he neared, he could make out some street people lingering there. He guessed he wouldn't stand out much after all.

Once inside the liquor store located on the corner, he'd slide over to the coolers to see what might be available. He changed his mind. A mom and pop grocery store sat next door. Some grocery stores didn't sell hard liquor or beer, so it was a gamble of sorts just to go in. He felt a pull toward the liquor store, but he knew this would present a different situation. It wouldn't be a subtle task to steal a bottle from the shelf.

As Nate passed the door, he was relieved to see a sign in the window of the grocery store advertising Heineken beer. It wasn't what he wanted, but it would hold him over until he could get some wine or whiskey. In he went. He stashed two bottles of Heineken under his shirt and looked around. Then he noticed a mother and her little boy in a stroller move toward the register. Nate moved past the register and out the door, heading back along the cracked walkway toward his current home on the tracks.

Someone had tossed a newspaper on the ground, or perhaps it had just blown in the wind and got caught in a nearby bush. Nate grabbed it. He wrapped the newspaper around the bottles and held the package under his arm.

Nate crossed the street and settled down in a large group of trees. Bending on one knee, he popped the cap off the first bottle. As he drank, he didn't care that his life was a mess.

# CHAPTER NINE

**B**aggage rolled off the conveyor belt and onto the baggage claim area. The usual impatient crowd of people waited to retrieve their luggage.

One by one, the passengers of Flight 641 picked up their suitcases and left the area. Tim Ford and his wife, Melissa, tried to spot their set of luggage.

"It's like a roulette wheel," he said, smiling.

Large windows lined one side of the roomy area and glared with the early sunlight. Through the windows they could see planes, jeeps, utility units, and various airport vehicles carrying on the usual operation of the airport. Flight 641 from San Francisco to Los Angeles had been uneventful and brought together a group of tourists whose ultimate destination was Las Vegas. The happy tourists formed a line that led to their chartered bus parked at the curb in front of the terminal.

The driver routed the group onto the bus, threw down the last of the storage doors, and climbed aboard. Thelma Thomas, the tour guide, separated vouchers from the tourist packets as she said, "I'll be your hostess all the way to Las Vegas, or as we say in this business, to the City of Lost Wages."

The tour bus rolled down the strip in Sin City and stopped in front a flashing sign that read, "Lots of Luck." The door opened with a *whoosh*, and Tim Ford stepped out onto the bottom step. A woman's voice filled the space around the tour bus thanks to a microphone.

"Anyone here wants to throw away their money, be my guest."

As if on cue, Ford reached into his wallet, pulled out a dollar bill, and tossed it in the air. Laughter could be heard from inside the bus.

* * *

Feeling scrubby and tired from scrounging for grub and wine, Nate walked up the street, stretching his arms and neck. He'd just left an alley and a smashed garbage can that he'd cracked over another bum's head minutes after an argument with the guy.

Adrenaline flowed, but he became calm as he walked. He shook his head in disbelief about his current circumstances. He rubbed the back of his knuckles as he turned on to the strip.

• • •

The dollar bill tossed from the tour bus dropped to the ground and lay next to the curb. A slight breeze moved it a foot or so to where Nate stood. He bent over and picked up the dollar. "Hey," he said with a halfhearted shout toward the moving bus. No one on board heard him. He pocketed the dollar bill. Then he walked into the Lots of Luck Casino. The dim light in the place met the sunlight as it snuck its way at an angle through the door, reflected off the top of a slot machine.

A few customers sat at the bar puffing on their smokes. The bartender looked up as he dried a glass. A rack of magazines and a phone booth stood by the bar. A cord from what once was attached to a phone swung back and forth with the light breeze that blew in through the door.

Nate exchanged the dollar bill, along with some spare change he had, for tokens at the bar and walked to the slot machine by the front door. He hesitated for a moment and then put a token in the slot machine and pulled the handle down. What did he have to lose?

The first few tokens brought only lemons to the screen. *So goes my life,* he told himself. With his last remaining token, he pulled the handle one more time. A black bar appeared in the first column. Another black bar showed in the second column. When the third column stopped spinning, a winning circle set off a blue light above the slot machine, and the loud clang of a bell filled Lots of Luck. Jackpot—twenty-five hundred dollars.

Nate stood there in a daze, frozen to the machine. His palms felt wet with sweat. In a split second, his thoughts rushed from scrounging for food on the streets of Las Vegas to what he would do with his winnings. The loud ringing of a bell signaled an attendant who hustled to the machine and Nate. The attendant looked over Nate for a moment as in disbelief. Then the casino worker plunked twenty-five one-hundred-dollar bills into Nate's trembling hands.

Gathering himself together, he left the casino bar without a thank you and headed down the street on the lookout for someone who might want to steal his fortune. A liquor store caught his attention. He rechecked his pockets for the money and crossed the street. A cheap bottle of wine would hit the spot.

Nate found what he was looking for. Two bucks for a cheap high wasn't a bad deal. He handed a one-hundred-dollar bill to the cashier, who examined the bill cautiously and then examined Nate. Nate left the store with his bottle of red wine and his change. In a discount clothing store not too far from the bar, Nate bought a pair of pants and a clean shirt. Now he felt he was back in business, the business of living. Tossing the clothes and wine together, he moved out to the street again.

This time, Nate walked with a little more confidence, pleased with the outcome of the last hour. He ducked into an alley, opened the bottle, and took a sip. The alleyway opened up to a rather expansive undeveloped area. He was sure he'd been there before, perhaps in a drunken stupor, because it all seemed so familiar.

A Dumpster lay overturned against the alley wall. On the other side, a gravel parking lot opened into a field of weeds. Row after row of shoddy box houses and colored blanket tents lined the field. A large barrel smoked from burning wood. The white smoke twisted into the air and dissipated into the late afternoon sky. An odd scent of garbage covered the camp.

Nate, drawn to the camp, approached the field, sat down, and shoved his clothes further into the bag as he tilted the bottle to his lips again. Not far from the edge of the camp, Nate noticed several men standing around. One man tended the smoking barrel and yelled profanities at a woman standing near a box house. He tossed a piece of wood into the barrel, and then he seemed to notice Nate. After a moment, he nodded to several of the men who turned to look at Nate. They motioned for Nate to join them. He responded with a nod and walked over.

Nate was no fool. He knew wine was the transient's only interest in him, and he wanted no part of that. Nate began to feel the shakes as he walked toward the smoking barrel. After a few sips of wine, surely after the whole bottle, he'd feel better. The guy who gestured to Nate shoved paper into the smoking barrel. The smell of paper mixed with wood filled the air before the fire sizzled, signifying its end. A final smoke curl danced up past his whiskered face and wrapped head and disappeared. The man coughed but still took out a cigarette butt and lit it with a piece of smoldering wood.

"How ya doin' there, bud?" he said to Nate.

Nate answered the man and then sipped his wine. The camp seemed comfortable and, in a peculiar way, Nate almost felt at home. He yawned and then coughed as a bit of smoke blew in his direction.

Some men had bandanas on their heads, unlike the women who wore wrapped rags atop their heads. Other men wore beat-up baseball caps while a few had no head covering to protect them from the overhead sun.

Nate took another swig of wine before he noticed that several of the men began to surround him. The congenial group changed now to a sudden and volatile situation. In the next instant, the men started to jeer at him and one pushed his arm. Before he knew it, the guy at the barrel drew a knife from out of nowhere and brandished it two inches from Nate's face.

Another guy drew a knife too. As the men surrounded him, the bandana head took a swipe at Nate, missing his face by a hair. With one fast move, Nate pushed away from the men and threw the wine bottle as hard as he could at the knife. Glass shattered and wine spilled over the guy's hand and head.

Nate shouted, "Keep your mitts off me. Get away from me. Don't touch me!" He fought his way through the snarling group. Angry with himself, he found an opening between two tents. In disbelief, Nate scrambled through the mess and found his bag of clothes. Just then, one of the men tried to tackle him, but Nate threw the man off his back and raced toward the alley.

# CHAPTER TEN

The Two Bit Flop House, a nickname used by itinerants for the Las Vegas Salvation Army Rescue Mission, was a two-story brick building, colorless, and empty looking from the outside. Inside, the top floor housed the indigent and neglected. Rows of cots filled the second floor. Nate's goal was to stay out of the place. Now, however, the rescue mission would be a good spot for him. Half aloud, he said, "Maybe I ought to try to sober up. That jerk almost stuck a knife in my face." Then, to himself he added, "At least the Rescue Mission was a place to flop, better than under a bridge, or sleeping on the ground."

Nate tossed his razor in the sink. The line was

long for the bathroom, but the wait was well worth it. He listened as a few men grumbled about the early morning wake-up call as they cleared their throats and spat. Some of them stretched and complained about their muscle stiffness while others remained quiet.

Except for occasional yelling from a few of the mission clients and the incessant snoring, Nate had spent a decent night. Once, a fellow in the cot next to him rolled over and tumbled on to the floor. The thud woke Nate. He helped the man back to his bed and tried to calm him down. The man shook from delirium tremens, the effects of alcoholism, and panicked until he fell back asleep.

Nate reached down, picked up, and then placed the razor on the sink's rim. He grabbed a plastic cup from the countertop, ripped the cover off, filled it, rinsed his mouth a few times, and swallowed. He looked like a different man after a shave, but he still had the face of a guy who ended up with a five o'clock shadow before midafternoon. He rubbed his cheeks with his hand and patted his face.

Nate decided to stay at the rescue mission for a few days to clean up. He knew he needed some time to sweat out the liquor and to rest.

The first day at the mission was long, boring, and hot. In the short hallway, someone had posted a bulletin board listing current jobs and rules. Everyone was expected to sign up for at least one task each

JOEY CHISESI AND DIANE CHISESI

day and to complete that task. All the clients were required to help in the kitchen in the basement.

Nate shook a little now and then. He could feel the booze leaving his body and knew it would take more than a couple days, but he was grateful for the start. The duties around the center would keep his mind off himself, keep him busy.

The current residents were also required to participate in at least one group meeting a day conducted by a team supervisor. If a person wanted to stay, he had to adhere to the objectives of the rescue mission. Nate attended his first meeting with the mission counselors a couple days after he arrived there.

The leader of his group was Captain James Swain. Swain spoke of his prior miserable existence and the fact that he was a former alcoholic. "I was a bum," he said. "I saw no hope for life. I was stranded in a sea of wine until I found God and his Son, Jesus Christ. It was through a mission like this one and its saving grace that I stand before you today, a happy man, a married man with children, a man with a new life. You can become what I've become. You can reject the life you've been leading. Let God and this mission do for you what another mission did for me."

The words somehow registered with Nate that day. He told himself, "It's time I start on a life path that leads to somewhere positive."

• • •  68  • • •

Most of the beds at the mission were filled each night. By midmorning, more than half of the people had left. The ever-present odor of the transients took a little getting used to, but after several days, Nate continued with the program and took note of a difference in himself.

Nate realized he didn't belong with the others. He found himself attending the meetings every day and moving further away from his bouts with alcoholism and closer to becoming a leader at the meetings, a role he relished.

A few days later, Captain Swain asked Nate to come into his office. "Have a seat, fellow. I've noticed you've been coming to the meetings. That's good. What's your name?"

"Nate."

"Nice to meet you, Nate."

"Where you from?"

"All over."

"Care to tell me a bit about yourself?"

Nate bent his head down.

"If you're not ready to talk about yourself, we can take these things slower. I sense you might have a bit of trust in us and what we do here. I see you're wearing new duds and you're clean shaved. That's a lot more than the most others we try to help here. You've also taken on some responsibilities in our Mission House. That's good Nate. That's real good.

That's the beginning of progress. Raise your head back up Nate. Endorse yourself."

Nate looked up at Swain. Swain took a handkerchief out of his pocket, rose from his chair, and walked a few steps to Nate. He put a firm hand on Nate's shoulder and handed Nate the handkerchief with his other hand.

"You know what, Nate? I think you need a friend. Something tells me that one of these days you'll want to tell me your life's story. I believe you've already lived a lifetime in your young years. I've got time to listen to you. I just know you've begun to listen to me. Will you come into my office tomorrow? How about two o'clock?"

Swain put out his hand toward Nate. He managed a bit of a smile and nodded. "Yeah, Captain, and thanks, thanks."

"No, Nate. Thank you."

. . .

A bakery in town delivered doughnuts and bagels to the mission each morning. The pastries arrived in plastic garbage bags. Nate's job was to open the bags and put the doughnuts and bagels on large plates. He also helped prepare food for at least one of the meals each day.

On his fifth day there, he recognized one or two of the transients who had returned for food.

By now, Nate was beginning to feel like one of the old hands. He slapped eggs and toast on someone's plate and shoved the spatula back into the pan.

Another two days went by before Nate started to talk to Captain Swain about himself. Nate insisted he'd not had much of a life to talk about. But Swain assured him once again that he did.

A few days following that session, Swain said to him, "You know, Nate, many men have led lives like yours, probably worse. Yet somehow they managed to rise above their misfortunes. I know this to be a fact. Would you believe you're talking with a man who hit bottom of the barrel at one point? Nate, I was so desperate; I thought about turning to crime, robbing banks, breaking into homes. I even considered suicide.

All this happened to me in Chicago. I slept on sidewalks just outside Chicago's downtown area. It's called skid row."

Nate let Captain Swain's words sink into his mind.

Captain Swain went on. "One day I was sitting on the sidewalk with my back against the brick wall of an empty storefront. A fellow came by me, looked down, and stopped. Lucky for me, I wasn't too drunk at the time.

"The man asked me if I'd like a drink. I thought he meant liquor, some kind of booze. Instead he said, 'Come with me.' I followed him. He led me to a rescue mission a couple blocks away. I resisted going in. He almost had to pull me inside. Yet, on the other hand, he was gentle. He insisted that I go through the doors of the mission. Maybe he was an angel. Maybe someone sent to help me.

"I stayed there a few months. The teams of volunteer workers kept reinforcing the idea that I needed to be there. It was a place like this—no bars on windows, no locked doors. I thought of walking away a few times, believe me. I'll bet any money you've had some of those thoughts since you've been here—"

"No, no. Honest I haven't had those thoughts." Nate interrupted him.

"It doesn't matter. Nate. What matters is you're here. You're welcome to stay as long as you wish. Believe it or not; you might say I graduated from the Mission House. I went much further; I started back to school. I studied human behavior. I worked and studied. And I got religion too. I became a believer. The man who led me there found a job for me. I put myself through college. I met my wife at work. And now, Nate, I'm blessed with two wonderful children.

"I became a volunteer at that same mission. Through the church I joined, well, the church asked me if I would come here, come to Las Vegas. My wife and I said yes.

"You see, Nate, there are good people in this

world. You need to seek them out. They're right here in this mission house. Not just the staff, but among our guests, our clients, as we call them. You're a good fellow, Nate. A good man. Let's work together. We'll help each other. You'll be good for my soul. I'm going to do my best to be good for yours."

Captain Swain's words found a place in Nate's heart and mind. Nate continued to make progress.

# CHAPTER ELEVEN

I n the past, Nate hadn't taken too much stock of his surroundings. He couldn't afford to. But now, after winning at the slot machine, volunteering at the mission house, and receiving counseling from Captain Swain, he felt like going to a gym he'd spotted two blocks from the mission.

Gerald's Place was a grimy, old boxing gym. Nate entered the gym one afternoon to look it over. It contained four boxing rings, one in each corner of the large training area. Boxers were sparring with partners in two of the rings, so Nate watched them for some time. Even though Nate had never boxed before, he felt he had a fast left hand and an even quicker right. He knew he was quick on his feet, athletic.

All around Nate, sweaty guys worked out. Jump ropes hung against a wall on one side. A few lay strewn on the floor, as did boxing gloves on a table at the back of the gym. In one corner a garbage can overflowed with trash.

Nate headed toward the back of the gym and walked into the owner's office. A man hung up the phone, looked at Nate, and said, "What can I do for you, son?"

Nate pointed out the open door behind him and said, "Those guys out there, I bet I could outfight them." He rubbed his knuckles.

"What's your name?"

Nate was awed by what he saw in the man's office. On the walls were portraits of world-famous boxers—Joe Lewis, Henry Armstrong, Jack Dempsey, Rocky Marciano, James J. Braddock, and Jake La Motta, among others. But he managed an answer. "Nate. Nate Bradford."

"You know, kid, I hear that line all the time. Well, let's see what ya got." He led Nate into the gym. "There're some gloves over there. Find a pair that fit ya, and we'll get ya wrapped up. Got some workout clothes, sweats, jock strap?" The man pulled the cigarette out of his mouth and smashed it under his foot.

"Nope, none of the above."

The man pointed to a storage locker. He handed Nate a key. "Go find what ya need in that pile of stuff in the locker room. They're all washed."

"Thanks," Nate said. He changed into some sweats and then warmed up on a punching bag. He danced around the bag and threw punches at the heavy sack. He started to break a sweat and to breathe heavy. Right then, he knew how out of condition he was.

Nate noticed that the owner stood in the middle of the gym overseeing four rings, but he concentrated on a sparring match in one ring in particular. He yelled at one of the fighters to keep his right up. Moments later, the boxer was sitting on the mat. The sparring match was over.

Nate stepped back from the bag to rest. There was a momentary silence in the gym as the owner hurried over to the ring to check on the downed boxer. He reached into his pants pocket, pulled out smelling salts, climbed through the ropes, and pushed the salts under the boxer's nose.

"Come on, kid. Open your eyes." He brushed the salts under the boxer's nose a second time and slapped his face as the boxer sat straight up. He turned to the boxer's opponent and yelled, "What the devil ya doin'? You're supposed to be sparring with each other. What ya trying to do, kill this guy?"

Nate threw a quick punch into the bag again. He hadn't looked at the boxer who took the punch.

Instead, he watched the other guy dance around the ring. With shiny forearms and strong, stern legs, the boxer punched his gloves together and shook his head back and forth in an almost wild manner. At one point, he caught sight of Nate. The two of them eyed each other.

Nate stared as the owner put the smelling salts back in his pocket and held the ropes open for the young fighter.

Nate went back to warming up with a few more jabs. Then he heard his name. "All right, Nate," the owner bellowed from across the gym. "Come here."

Nate gave the bag one more solid punch and sauntered over to where the man stood.

"I'll give ya' a few days to get loosened up, get your licks up. Then I'll stick ya in on Thursday for a sparring match with José. I'm Maxwell, by the way."

"Okay, Mister Maxwell."

"Max to you. Everyone calls me Max. Some call me Max the Axe behind my back."

"Yes, sir."

"You look like you might be able to handle yourself real good, kid," Max said. "But you look out of shape despite your boasting."

Nate hung his head.

"Tell ya what. Come back tomorrow and continue workin' out, if you can raise your arms, that is. You're a good lookin' kid. I don't want your face to get cut up. I'm just watchin' out for you. That's

JOEY CHISESI AND DIANE CHISESI

my job. What do ya weigh? One seventy? One seventy-five?"

Nate nodded.

"I'll put you on the scale tomorrow. Yeah, you'll probably box as a light heavyweight. Check back with me later, and we'll go over the paperwork."

With that, Max hustled toward his office.

Now in his fifties, Max had had more fights in his boxing past than any of his fighters could imagine they'd ever have. His gym had thrived through ups and downs in the business world. His fighters were hungry, eager to claim purses for each fight they'd have. Max's job was to get matches for his fighters and train each fighter to the keenest degree, hoping for bigger and more lucrative rewards.

Nate found a water bottle, took a swig, and squirted the rest over his head.

. . .

It was late on a Tuesday evening as Nate readied to leave Gerald's Place. He felt satisfied with the day's progress. He flirted with the idea of winning a few dollars as a professional fighter.

The day before, Nate told Captain Swain about his meeting with Max the Axe. He told him about his desire to become a professional boxer. Captain Swain wasn't thrilled with the thought. "Well, it isn't exactly my cup of tea, Nate. I guess you know that. But if you do follow this up, keep everything you do clean, above board. I guess maybe you can call being a fighter an athlete and boxing a career. You sure will have to keep your body in good shape. At least it's a step forward. You're showing me you have ambition. I'd hope now you keep your mind and you're inner soul in good shape at the same time. Please stay here with us. Serve God while you start to conquer the world."

Nate thought about what the captain said, and then he threw a towel against the wall and watched it fall on a pile of towels next to the lockers. Nate pulled his shirt off and wrung it under a faucet for a few minutes. He tossed it around his shoulders and headed for the exit.

As he moved through the gym, passing the boxing rings and punching bags, he began to realize he had potential as a human being, something he'd buried for far too long.

A wave of warm air hit Nate when he stepped outside. The lights of Vegas had started to take over the impending darkness. The sounds of the city joined them. Nate smiled and then headed toward the mission. Time for something to eat.

# CHAPTER TWELVE

**N**ate picked up a roll, grabbed more mashed potatoes, and piled them on his plate. Every now and then the food at the mission was decent. He grabbed a toothpick from a jar, trying to remember the last time he'd had roast beef and gravy for dinner.

Tomorrow, he figured, he'd head to the library when his shift in the kitchen was over. Today, he figured he'd buy some new duds, maybe even get a haircut.

In the morning, Nate went to the main branch of the Las Vegas Public Library. Sunlight cut through the library's front window as Nate headed to the main desk, concentrating on what book he'd ask the librarian for. A woman with a bag tucked under her right arm and a book in her other hand turned right into Nate.

Nate and the woman bumped right into one and another. Surprised and startled, they looked at each other. Then they both laughed.

"I'm so sorry," Nate said. "Here, let me help you with that." He bent to pick up her book and handbag. The woman picked up her purse and held it to her side as she rose from a squatting position. She was shorter than Nate.

Nate didn't know where it came from, but he said, "Let me buy you a drink, a cup of coffee,"

The woman seemed coy. "Is this your run-of-the mill way to meet someone?"

"You think I bumped into you on purpose? Really, I think you bumped into me."

She shrugged.

"Actually, the sun blinded me for half a second," Nate said, letting the woman win that quick discussion.

"Sure, I'll take you up on the coffee. I work over at the reference desk, but I'll take my break in a half hour or so. I'll see you at the coffee stand next door. I'm Misty."

"I'm Nate."

# CHAPTER THIRTEEN

M ax's arena seated about four thousand people. It stood next to Gerald's Place. Max took the opportunity to expose boxers to a variety of competitors, one of which would be Nate. Max had been impressed during the last few weeks with the kid's raw talent. The kid had done well with his sparring and training. Max decided to bring him over to the bigger venue.

Before each fight, gamblers bet based on the odds established earlier in the day. The odds could change, however, right up to the start of each fight. The amount of the purse for each boxer was set by signed contracts of win, lose, or draw. Max set the purse by those contracts.

Max oversaw the boxers at this level, so they had one fight per month after qualifying in a sparring event. Nate soon qualified for his first fight for a purse after six weeks of torturous training.

Nate entered the ring. He punched his gloves together and wiped the Vaseline off his brow that had dripped into his eyes. Hunching his shoulders together, he threw a few punches into the air. The announcer, doing his best to sound impressive, began the introduction.

Nate's heart pounded with excitement as the announcer bellowed over the microphone, "We welcome you to Max the Axe's arena for a rousing evening of boxing presented by Maxwell White Promotions. This is the first of six fights on tonight's card. But first, let's all sing the national anthem. To lead us tonight will be the talented singer, Miss Sally Troth."

Troth sang an a cappella rendition of "The Star Spangled Banner" unaccompanied because 95 percent of the fight fans just stood there with their hands over their hearts and left the singing to her.

As she sang, Nate danced in his corner while a calm Hernando Caesar Lopez stared at him. This unnerved Nate, but he tried to keep his focus and remember what Max had taught him from the very first day he walked into Gerald's Place.

JOEY CHISESI AND DIANE CHISESI

Ring announcer Davey Jacobs resumed his introductions. "And now, in the corner to my left, taking part in his very first professional fight, wearing purple trunks with a white stripe, and hailing from Seattle, Washington, is Nate 'The Wanderer' Bradford."

A slight applause followed.

"And in the corner to my right, wearing gold trunks with a black stripe is the popular Las Vegas puncher, Hernandoooo Caesar Looopez." His fans clearly outnumbered Bradford's.

"Refereeing tonight's four-round contest will be the former great welterweight contender from Henderson, Nevada, Creighton … Toughie … Johnson." Johnson nodded his head toward the spectators. Jacobs continued. "The three-knockdown rule will be in effect." Then he introduced the ringside judges.

Referee Johnson motioned to both fighters to come to the center of the ring and gave them their instructions. Nate knew them because Max had drummed them into his head. At the end of his instructions, Johnson told the fighters, "Shake hands and come out fighting."

Nate and Lopez returned to their corners. Max shoved Nate's mouthpiece into place. The warning buzzer sounded, followed in ten seconds by the clang of the bell. The fight began.

Nate moved around the ring as the two of them

• • • 84 • • •

felt each other out. They danced through the first two rounds. The crowd booed. The fighters were in the third round of their four-round contest when Nate, breathing hard, wondered if he would have to go the distance with his opponent. He made it through the third round unscathed, except for tiring.

Between rounds, Max worked on Nate, gave him water to rinse his mouth, and told him, "Kid, you're behind on my scorecard and on the judge's scorecard too. You gotta take this guy out this round. You don't have but three minutes left to do the job. Get mad, kid. Get mad, like you told me you used to on the street. This guy ain't your sister. Get mad!"

The bell rang for round four. The referee bade each fighter to touch gloves for the final three minutes of the bout. After a wave from the referee, the two boxers pounded on each other with a flurry of punches. Nate realized Lopez was working his arms and hitting with fewer body punches. This could work to Nate's advantage. Nate's upper body strength kept him moving in spite of Lopez's shots.

Lopez tagged Nate across the chin. The punch surprised Nate. Then Nate's survivor mode kicked in, and in an instant, Nate followed Lopez toward the ropes and waited as Lopez tried to reverse his stance. Nate repositioned his right shoulder, kept his right up by his face, and jabbed with his left. Then he faked a left and Lopez fell for it.

With one quick shot, Nate landed a firm punch that cut Lopez's eye. Blood spurted across Lopez's face. He dropped to the canvas.

The referee started to count over Lopez, but Lopez got to his feet. At this point, the referee signaled time-out and led Lopez to his corner.

A ringside doctor examined the cut and signaled okay. The referee waved both fighters to resume. Nate wasn't going to be stopped now. He pummeled Lopez with punches until the referee threw his arms around Lopez and signaled the end of the fight. Almost a minute was left in the final round.

Nate felt a little more composed as he made a quick check of the front rows of the arena to see if the gal he met at the library, Misty, was there. She was.

The microphone was lowered to Jacobs. "The winner, by technical knockout at two minutes into the fourth and final round: Nate 'The Wanderer' Bradford!" Referee Johnson held Nate's right arm up. The crowd cheered.

# CHAPTER FOURTEEN

**M**isty had never been to a prizefight. She was anything but thrilled with the fact that her new beau was into boxing—such a brutal sport. Max had her sit in the third row as a favor to Nate; too close, as far as she was concerned. She didn't need to see the blood and gore.

The fight was over. Thank goodness. She smiled back as Nate caught her attention. Max flew into the ring and pulled Nate back to his corner. The ref followed, grabbed Nate's arm, and held it in the air once more to indicate the win. Then Max moved Nate around the ring as they acknowledged shouts from the crowd.

Misty remained seated. Should she wait for him there? Or try to find him in the dressing rooms? She sighed.

"Let's get these gloves off ya and we'll talk in the back. Way to go, Nate," Max said. "Lopez's not someone to take lightly!" He parted the ropes. Nate slipped through and jumped down to the floor.

"Get washed up. Your purse brought in a grand. Not a bad way to make a quick buck, huh?"

While Nate dressed, Max told him how close he had come to losing the fight. "If you're interested, I got two or three more fights lined up. Oh, by the way, I bet some dough on ya. You were the underdog. I won big. I got six to one odds. I'm throwing an extra five hundred bucks in yer purse, for you. You earned it, kid. You earned it."

Nate thumbed through the bills Max stuffed in his palm.

"Sure thing, Max. Yeah, I'm interested." Nate caught sight of Misty through the narrow gap in the door. "Oh, and thanks, Max. I really needed this fight."

"No problem, kid. Come back in a day or two and I'll have dates and times for the next few fights."

"You bet." Nate grabbed a sport coat and headed out the door toward Misty.

Nate took Misty by the arm. "Let's get out of this joint," he said. As the evening wore on, Nate decided to go to a restaurant for a quick bite of dinner. As they ate, he began to tell Misty more about his past life. Misty nibbled at a BLT sandwich.

She listened without comment for a while. Then Misty said, "You know, you're not the same man I met a month ago. It makes me feel good to know you're comfortable talking to me about yourself, and I want you to know I'm proud of you, Nate, but I'm really scared. The man I saw win a fight tonight and the man you are at this moment just don't add up. You're meant for better things. I don't think you belong in the fighting world. You're a decent man, Nate. You know this, don't you?"

Misty's words almost brought tears to Nate's eyes.

# CHAPTER FIFTEEN

I t was evident to Nate that his life had changed by great leaps and bounds. Processing the change was unimportant to him, but the significance of the change was.

Crumpled in one of his pants pockets was a note regarding work in the area. He jotted down a few names and numbers on a clean piece of paper and stuffed it into his pocket for later. Nate enjoyed boxing, but in the back of his mind, he wondered if this kind of life was the path he'd choose for his future.

Nate wanted to have children someday and knew time wouldn't always be his friend. One thing was certain. He was cleaning up his life. Not only had he picked himself up from the streets, but he'd found reason to keep moving in the right direction, or at least the direction he believed was the right one for now.

The business of being a professional boxer was not an easy life. It was brutal, calculating, and unforgiving. One mistake could put him in the hospital, or worse, in a pine box. He thought about the distinction between fighting for a person's life and fighting for money. At the moment, though, there was no difference to him except for one thing: Misty.

While Misty and his relationship were still new, it had begun to play an important role in his life. Nate found Misty different from other women he had known. The very thought of her excited him. Not like a boxing match or a fight on the street but in a different way. He couldn't quite figure out what was going on between them, but he knew it was something he didn't want to change.

A month went by of heavy training. Nate's days became patterned: get to the gym, work out, visit with Misty as often as he could. His muscles became firm, molded into a single unit of athletic perfection, a sculptor's dream. Modest as he was, he had to admit to admiring himself in front of a mirror.

About his change, Nate credited his sessions at the rescue mission too. They were like Alcoholics Anonymous but with a lot of emphasis on religion.

He admitted his love for Misty, his fondness for Max. All were making him into a different man.

Max had begun to replace Nate's father, if that could have been possible. Misty, in turn, provided the inspiration for Nate's soul along with Swain, the mission captain. Now, more than ever before, Nate saw himself as a man of pride. He drifted further and further away from the belligerent being he had been.

And so, Max called Nate into his office. Max asked him if he'd like a second fight.

Nate jumped at the opportunity.

On a Monday morning, Max said, "Okay, kid, you'll be on my fight card this coming Friday night. Work hard this week and get ready."

Nate used the phone on Max's desk to call Misty. "Max got me another fight."

Misty didn't speak at first. Then she said, "Honey, I know how hard you've worked out, but I'm afraid of you being injured. Are you sure this is what you want to do?"

# CHAPTER SIXTEEN

**F**riday fight night arrived. Nate entered the arena, walked into the dressing room, stripped his clothes off, put on his boxing trunks, and hung his street clothes in a locker. He could hear Max shouting from the other room. "Get your gloves on, Nate! What's taking you so long?"

"No problem, Max. On my way."

Max had a routine he liked his boxers to follow prior to a match. Nate wasn't opposed to it, but he wasn't real fond of taking harsh orders. However, Max insisted. He expected his boxers to warm up and get loose. It wasn't a strange request. In fact, everyone knew that if his boxers failed to follow his orders, the match wouldn't start. He'd been known to cancel a fight minutes before it was to start.

Nate eyed some of the fighters on the night's card. He took a pair of boxing gloves from Max's office locker and threw them over his shoulder. Nate wore dark navy trunks with a white stripe down each side.

He and the other boxers warmed up, creating an atmosphere for the evening, an evening paced with excitement. Max pruned his boxers like a landscape artist shaped his shrubs.

The lights in the arena settled in a dull glow, forming peculiar shadows on the green trimmed walls. People walked around the fight arena as they waited for the first fight to begin.

Nate was again scheduled for the first fight. A strong opening fight on an evening's fight card helped set the stage for the remainder of the program. Max provided the fight fans with just that. He whistled for Nate to head his way. Nate responded with a nod and started across the arena toward the ring.

Max parted the ropes and Nate stepped through. He bounced around on the mat a few times and punched his fists together. He seemed to be in a different mood this night. Nate headed for his corner.

Once again, Max was by his side. Max checked and double-checked the grease on Nate's shoulders and then patted Nate on the face a few times.

He insisted Nate focus and look at him straight

in the eye. Max held up one finger and brought it toward Nate's forehead.

"Pay attention. When I tell you to do something, do it. Understood?"

Nate agreed and accepted the instructions. "Let our cut guy, Bernie, handle your body. You listen to me for instructions. Ya got it, kid?"

Nate's fight was against Reggie Bouilli, a Frenchman from Canada. He too was somewhat new to the Las Vegas boxing circuit. But Bouilli had already created a small following of people who shouted to him from the back of the arena.

The usual pre-fight festivities took place. Nate stood with Max at his back as he turned to face his opponent. The referee commanded the men to come to the center of the ring for instructions.

The warning buzzer sounded, followed by the bell for the start of the first round.

Nate came out punching, hit Bouilli in the side, and then hit him with a fast uppercut to the head. With remarkable speed and power, Nate pounded Bouilli for a few seconds. Sweat rolled off Nate. He had caught Bouilli off guard. Bouilli stepped back and brought his arms up in a defensive position. Nate scored points.

Bouilli wasn't a patient boxer. After seeming to feel the strength of his opponent, he took a few heavy breaths. He was angry now, something he was well known for.

Nate was fueled by his survivor mechanism. The difference between the two boxers made this fight more intense than the usual opening bout at the arena. The bell rang, ending the first round. Nate and Bouilli withdrew to their corners.

"Don't overdo it these first couple rounds, kid. He's quick and fast and just as strong as you. Look at me now. Settle down," Max commanded.

Nate took some water as Max poured a few drops into his mouth. Then Max shoved his fighter's mouthpiece back into place. "Settle down," Max insisted.

Nate felt his chest rise and fall and his heart speed up as if it might jump out of his body. He moved his head back and forth and side to side. Nate raised his shoulders in a stretching motion as he stood up. Max pulled the corner stool under the ropes and stepped back away from the ring as the bell sounded for round two.

The second round saw both fighters turn conservative and score points. Both showed a remarkable amount of stamina that brought them to the third round.

In the third round, they were fighting in a neutral corner on the ring ropes. Nate kept Bouilli in front of him, punching away at Bouilli's forearms and stomach. Bouilli was beginning to lower his arms. Nate saw this and pounded him through the remainder of the third round. The fans applauded.

Max gave Nate a light slap on the face. "Listen to me. I don't want this fight going any longer. You finish this guy off right away. Got me, kid?"

Nate nodded in agreement. He was winded but holding strong. He knew he had Bouilli tired. Nate pooled all his mental resources and stood ready for the fourth round.

The noise in the arena grew louder as onlookers shouted their approval.

As if for more incentive, Max reminded Nate that Nate was the underdog; more gamblers had bet on Bouilli.

The crowd was surprised at Nate's ability, considering this was only his second fight.

Nate had decided even before Max's instructions to end the fight right after the bell for the fourth and final round.

Nate pounded Bouilli with so much force that Bouilli's legs began to quiver. Nate attacked him like an animal coming in for a kill. Bouilli backed into the ropes with his hands up by his face, and Nate slammed lefts and rights into Bouilli's stomach. Bouilli, totally winded, tried to move off the ropes to the center of the ring, but it was too late. Nate hit him with a devastating right hand into his gut and then, with full force, caught Bouilli square on the side of his face.

Bouilli's mouthpiece squirted out from his mouth

and fell to the mat. A second later, he dropped to the canvas. He was out cold.

The referee could have counted to twenty if need be, but that was it. The fight was over.

Nate bounced around the ring, still punching his gloves together. With the help of his seconds, Bouilli got up from the canvas. The referee spread his arms out, putting one arm over Bouilli as if to protect him from further punishment.

Max leaped into the ring and grabbed Nate. "That's it! The fight's over!"

Nate, still pumped with adrenaline, pulled back from Bouilli. The referee followed Max's voice. "It's all over, son. It's over!"

In a few moments, Nate crossed over to his opponent's corner, touched him in a gentleman's manner, and wished him well.

# CHAPTER SEVENTEEN

Later that night, Nate held Misty in his arms. She lifted her hand and caressed his face. Troubled by the bruises on his cheeks and his puffed eyes, she stared at him.

"How long are you going to keep fighting, Nate?"

"As long as it takes me to get myself back on my feet. Now, tell me, why all the questions?"

"I care about you. I know boxing is a rough business, that's all." She kissed him.

Nate took both of Misty's arms and put them around his neck. He reached around her thighs and pulled her close to his body.

"Do you know I have almost six thousand dollars? Not bad, wouldn't you say? I can't stay at the mission much longer. Maybe I should have left there after the first couple of weeks. I need to find something better, something more respectable."

"What do you mean?"

"Well, I'd like to stay right near Gerald's Place. Find a place so I can walk to the gym and be close to your apartment too. That's my idea right now, but I want to visit with Captain Swain whenever I get the chance."

Misty nodded her head.

The two had difficulty staying away from each other. Both restrained themselves from daily visits, resorting to phone calls, almost like teenagers in high school. That kind of teen joy had passed Nate by.

Misty had been elected homecoming queen of her senior class and was as much an excellent student as she was a pretty young lady. She had studied hard in college in hope of landing a position as head librarian somewhere. After graduating from Sierra Community College in Rocklin, California, she earned her teaching degree at the University of California, Davis. U C Davis wasn't too far from her home. She lived with her dad at his home in Newcastle on his vineyard and winery. Job opportunities opened for her, and she chose the assistant head librarian's post at the Las Vegas City Library. Misty Wakefield was proud of her position. She loved her work.

Nate's sobering up process, now past and under control, dictated his behavior. Three people he idolized were responsible for his progress—Max, Misty, and Captain Swain.

Nate and Misty found him a two-room furnished apartment close to Misty's apartment and the gym. He said his good-byes to Captain Swain and other staff members at the mission. Misty continued her campaign against Nate's boxing career, but she was careful not to be too insistent, not to threaten Nate with her words.

# CHAPTER EIGHTEEN

And then Max offered Nate his third opportunity in the form of a fight with José "Jamie" Flores, a veteran fighter who still carried an ambition to rise in the professional ranks. Stepping down to fight a young warrior with only two previous fights would not boost any fighter's career, but Nate's name had surfaced in the sports section of the local newspapers. Nate's star was rising. The scuttlebutt around Vegas said, "This guy is one to watch. He's got fists of steel, a real comer."

It was now four months since their chance meeting in the library. Misty voiced her usual concerns.

"Mist, I know I'll be okay. What skills do I have

other than boxing? Max is going to up my take to four thousand for my fight with Flores. I tell you what. After this fight, we'll sit down and talk about my future."

Nate kept talking. "I'm not too old to finish college. I figure I might be able to major in teaching, probably in the athletic department. Max taught me a lot and so have you. I've learned about a better life, and I know I've finally gotten rid of my past. I want to make you proud of me, so proud you'll burst your buttons. Just kidding! But I've got to get on with my life. Go forward. Hang in there with me through this fight, okay? Maybe you can come and watch, even though it's tough on you. Mist, if you sit way back in the last row or so, it'll be easier on you. When you sit up close, well, I got to admit, that's rough."

When Nate was about ten years old, his folks took him and his sister to Hawaii for a two-week vacation. They spent one of those weeks on Kauai near the village of Princeville. They stayed in a condo with a balcony that overlooked Hanalei Bay and Bali Hai of the musical South Pacific fame.

That vacation was stamped forever in Nate's mind. The beauty of the ocean as it rolled onto the sandy shore and the clouds that drifted across the sky made the mountain even more three-dimensional.

Nate remembered he was having fun feeding a dove that returned at the same time every day. The dove cocked its head and looked at Nate as he gave it some cereal flakes. Then the dove seemed to sense something else and flew away, never to return the rest of the week.

This memory of Hawaii did a ballet through Nate's mind. Misty had become his Hawaiian paradise. Her beauty was as fragile to him as a dove. Every time his hands touched her lovely face, he tried to tell her, "Do you understand what you've come to mean to me, Misty? Can you see the picture I see in my mind?"

# CHAPTER NINETEEN

Misty began to question if she had the right to urge Nate to drop his pugilistic career, to quit the ring. Her instinct told her Nate had what it took to succeed. She just had to decide if she wanted to be with him while he struggled to get there.

Misty prayed for Nate to give up his quest for money and fame, the kind a prizefighter sought. Imbedded in her mind was the hope he'd shed his boxing gloves and leave that battleground of physical brutality. She couldn't get out of her mind the possibility that Nate's subconscious still admonished him for his past indiscretions.

"But when do you forgive yourself?" she said aloud.

"Misty, are you okay? Is something bothering you?" an assistant librarian, Sue Ellen said.

"Oh no, not really. I guess I was just thinking about something."

"Or someone. Were you thinking about your guy?"

"Yes, I was thinking about Nate. I'll tell you all about it sometime."

"You can't fool me, Misty. I know you're different."

"Do you read tea leaves too?" Misty smiled.

"Hey, girl, I'm your friend, ain't I?"

"That's terrible English for a librarian. And, yes, you're a good friend. I was just thinking aloud."

"You mean wishing aloud, don't you?"

"Okay, okay. You're right. I was wishing aloud."

"You're not, you know what I mean. You're not that way, are you?"

"Sue Ellen, I'm shocked. Of course not! Nate's never made an inappropriate move. Besides, I have a moral code I live by. So does Nate."

"Sorry, Misty. I guess I really meant that you seem so happy since you met him."

"Of course I am. You bet. I just worry about his work."

"You mean fighting? That's work all right. That's for sure. George and I saw his second fight on TV. Lord. We were stunned. I can see how you would be on pins and needles while he's in the ring. I know I'd be."

A library guest approached Misty at that point with a question. The subject of Nate would have to wait.

# CHAPTER TWENTY

**H**is third bout neared, and Nate felt sharper than he imagined he'd ever be as he drilled the punching bags with precision and rhythm, playing a staccato beat.

Far too young to have known the days of former heavyweight champion Mohammad Ali, he'd read about Ali in the library when Misty found books for him about famous boxers.

Nate read about Ali's saying, "Float like a butterfly and sting like a bee." He started to drill the speed bag now with that quotation in his mind. He'd pound the body bag with devastating force, pretending he was hitting his opponent in the stomach and upper chest. *Pow, pow, pow.*

Nate jogged for miles, seldom needing to open his mouth for air.

Two days before the fight, Nate noticed Max paying more attention to him than the other fighters in his stable. As afternoon rolled into evening, Nate and Max took a break. A few boxers continued their workouts at the punching bags. Another struggled with a universal bar set. Otherwise, the gym was quiet.

"So, kid, what's going on with this gal ya been seeing?" Max said between swigs of coffee. "You seem preoccupied. Everything hunky dory?"

"As a matter of fact, I was just thinking about Misty. Yeah, sure, everything's fine. Super, in fact."

"I figured. Your head sure seems to be someplace else."

Max slapped Nate on the back. "Come on, kid, have a cup of coffee."

Nate reached for the pot. He didn't care much for coffee, but if Max told him to have a cup, he'd better have one.

"This woman struck a note with ya, hasn't she?" Max said. He continued to prod Nate about Misty. He said, "I don't want you overwhelmed with this gal. Remember, you came up from the gutter. You don't want to slip back there, do ya?"

Then he said, "But, kid, there's nothing wrong with ya' fallin' in love."

Nate didn't respond, but the words tumbled

around in his mind as Max spoke. God, yes. He'd fallen in love with Misty. No doubt now. Wasn't this the way life was supposed to be? Wasn't this as natural as early morning sunrays? When he and Misty were together, everything meshed.

In his mind, Nate went over how they completed each other's sentences and how she seemed to listen without judging him. And how much they respected each other.

Another month went by. Nate trained as hard as he could. He punished his body, toned his body to show Max how he could be a better, more rugged fighter. As a result, Max promised Nate a bigger purse.

. . .

Max watched Nate leave his desk and jab at a heavy bag as he headed for the speed bag. Max would hate to lose a guy like Nate. This kid was a natural: his stance, his moves, his fighting animal instinct.

As Max watched, Nate tattooed the speed bag with a series of machine gun intervals. Nate tried to wipe the sweat off his face with his boxing gloves. Then he hit the bag one more time before he picked up a jump rope. He looped the rope around his back and sped through his workout. He looked at the clock again just as he'd done before he grabbed the

A DOLLAR'S WORTH

jump rope, Max noted. After a little footwork, Nate headed for the showers.

Max noticed the absence of echoes in the gym. Even though he preferred to keep the gym operating all night while his boxers trained, it felt good to have a reprieve. He began his routine of shutting down the gym for another day.

Nate hollered for Max to let him out. Max pulled the heavy metal doors shut behind Nate. Nate wasn't gone but a few moments when there was a pounding on the doors.

Max heard two guys yelling at him to open up. Max did. "What do you creeps want?"

"Cool it, Max. We need to talk. You could use some extra dough, couldn't ya?"

"Naw. Nobody needs extra dough, 'specially me. I'm askin' you again. What the devil do you want?"

"Just like you, Max, we're after extra bucks."

"What's this? A stickup? I'm askin' ya once more. What are you after?""

"We got a deal for ya, Max. A deal. Ya like to deal, don't ya?"

"With punks like you? I don't want to deal with you slobs. Who sent you?"

"You know who sent us. Our boss, that's who sent us."

"Yeah, I think I know your boss. He's no good. Neither are you two flunkies."

"Cool it, Max. Your kid's new. So he takes a

● ● ● 111 ● ● ●

dive. So what? No one'll know. New kids lose all the time. Got it, Max? You can teach him how to take a fall. The kid's a bum anyway."

Max had to restrain himself. He was filled with rage. "You cheap, miserable punks. Get out of here and don't come back. Go on; scram. Beat it. Here's the door. Get out of here and fast. Get out of my gym."

Max shoved the two guys through the doorway, closed it again, and took out a cigarette. He knew who the creeps were after all right. He vowed to call the Nevada Boxing Commissioner's office the next morning. He also told himself not to say a word about the incident to Nate.

# CHAPTER TWENTY-ONE

On the way to the arena, Nate stopped at the library to speak to Misty.

"Hey, Mist, I know you're worried about me. In a way, that makes me feel good."

"You're darn right I'm worried about you. I couldn't eat a thing today. Am I not supposed to be worried?"

"Hey, girl, I hate to see you worry over a dumb thing like a prizefight."

"Prizefight? Who ever labeled the barbarity of fighting a prizefight? It's more like a slaughterhouse."

"Heck, look at me. Look at these muscles. You got to worry about the dude getting into the ring with me. That's who you need to worry about.

Come on, Misty. Come to the fight with me tonight, honey."

"I can't, Nate. I just can't bear to see you get hurt like that. You understand, don't you? Please don't pressure me."

"Aw, girl. I was just hoping. Tell you what I'll do. I'll knock this guy out in the first round. Get it over quick. I won't have a mark on me. You watch. I'll be at your apartment by eight thirty tonight. We'll celebrate with a banana split. Hey, you know what? I can't remember when I last had one of those things. How's that grab you, baby?"

"You've got a deal, honey. I'll be praying for you and for the other guy too. What's his name?"

"The bum's name is Flores, Jamie Flores. Mist, you're a saint. I care about you, sweetie! I just plain care."

Nate threw Misty a kiss. He walked the three blocks to the arena, headed for the dressing room, and readied for his fight against Flores.

At eight thirty sharp, Nate rang Misty's bell from the lobby of her building. She didn't bother to ask who was there.

When he knocked on her second-floor apartment door, Misty looked at Nate and said, "What happened? Did they cancel the fight? You don't have a mark on you!"

"Let me tell you, Mist, I canceled the fight. I canceled it in the first round. I canceled Flores!"

"I don't understand. What does that mean?"

"Misty, gal, I knocked the bum out in the first round. He never had a chance. Didn't I tell you I'd do that?"

"Good Lord. You really did, didn't you?"

"Yep, and I'm four grand richer than I was a couple hours ago. Let's get that banana split. I'm buying."

Nate had charged Flores right from the sound of the bell, battered him with lefts and rights before Flores could react. The fight fans in the audience roared their approval. They never expected to see a first-round knockout, especially the first minute of the first round.

Flores's handlers stared at Nate in amazement and anger. Then when Flores recovered his senses in a few minutes, they helped him climb through the ropes and walk out of the ring on his own.

# CHAPTER TWENTY-TWO

**B**oth Nate and Misty continued to draw closer to each other. If there were any contentious moments, they appeared when she shared her feelings about the brutality of prizefighting.

To counter, Nate would show up at the library, take a book from a shelf, and absorb himself in the text. He no longer just read about boxing. Instead he studied books on physical fitness. Once in a while, he'd study American history.

Late one Friday afternoon, Misty handed him a book on grape growing and wine making. Never one to be quiet in the library, he joked about her giving him such a subtle hint.

"Are you looking at a retirement plan for me, baby? I have the world in the palm of my hand, Mist. Look at this body."

"Sshhh," she whispered to him. "Nate, you've got to come back to earth. Simmer down a bit."

"Hey, baby, I've got some big news for you. Let's go jogging tomorrow morning. We'll take a ride out east where we can run up and down the hills. I want to show you some fancy homes out that way. Deal? Pick me up at nine."

Misty nodded. "Okay, if you promise to read this book for an hour or so."

"Yes, teacher," Nate said as he bowed before her desk. He winked at her and found a chair at a reference table. An hour or so later, he gave her back the book and said, "I'm going to start a distillery in my apartment. I'll keep the wine in my bathtub."

"Yes, and I'll recruit customers for you from the mission house."

"Ouch, honey. I got the message. Oh, by the way, we're having dinner out tonight at the Casino Royale."

"Not Burger King? We're beginning to look like hamburgers."

" Ouch. That's two jabs today. Just for that, pick me up at seven. We're going out first class tonight. We're switching to Wendy's."

He blew her the usual kiss and headed for the exit door.

Sue Ellen had watched Nate and Misty from her desk next to Misty. She giggled and blew a kiss at Misty the same way Nate had.

Misty thumbed her nose at Sue Ellen and grinned.

At a few minutes after seven, Misty pulled into the parking area at Nate's apartment. He pointed to his watch. "You're six minutes late. I suppose you had to fight off a pack of dudes before you got here."

Misty laughed. "I've picked up all my martial arts training from you. Now, I'm not afraid of anyone, as long as you're around, that is. Come to think of it, that's one advantage of dating a prizefighter. Maybe the only one."

"Hey, sweetie pie, come upstairs a minute. Something I want to show you."

They climbed the three flights of stairs to Nate's apartment.

"Close your eyes and don't open them till I say so." He went to his closet and brought out a new suit he'd bought at Sears.

"Okay, open your eyes."

"Oh, Nate, it's beautiful. Now you have to get a new shirt and a nice blue tie. I bet you'll look great in it."

"Don't mind telling you I do. I had to battle my way past the lady clerks when I tried it on at the store. They made me sign autographs too. Well, at least one—the sales slip, that is. But you'll see. Soon, I'll be signing autographs for hundreds of people."

With that, he went back to the closet and came out with a bouquet of red and white carnations.

"Oh, honey, they're lovely," Misty said. "Let's put them in some water. Find me a tall glass or a vase, will you?"

"Vase? Are you kidding?"

As they left Nate's apartment, Misty asked him where they were eating. Nate said, "Casino Royale, like I told you in the library."

"There's no Casino Royale in Vegas, but there is a Wendy's."

"Yeah, and a Burger King too." He paused for a moment. "I have reservations at the Venetian."

"The Venetian?"

"You bet. We're dining in the Taqueria Canonita restaurant. Right where they have a canal and gondoliers sing. Just like Venice, Italy. Ever been there before? I mean the restaurant? I almost forgot the name of the restaurant for a moment. That's it though, the Taqueria Canonita. I worked on the pronunciation all day. It's funny, a Mexican restaurant by the canal they built there. I think it should be Italian food. I've got us a reservation for a boat ride too!"

"Nate, you're so excited. You're kidding me."

"No, I'm serious. We have reservations to do both, baby."

"What a wonderful surprise. Oh, sweetheart, you're the best guy ever. Well, next to my dad, of course."

"Hey, I don't want to be second string to any-body, not even your daddy!"

"Tough, buddy. That's how it is."

"Well, all right, just to your old man."

The two of them made light conversation until they found their way to the restaurant and were seated. Nate refused an offer to order wine, but he suggested Misty order for them. She too said no. In the middle of their dinner, Nate began a serious conversation.

"Honey, Max called me into his office today and we had a long talk. Now, bear with me here. Just listen to this."

"I know what you're going to tell me already. He wants you to fight another guy. Am I right?

"Yep, you're right. But listen, please, to this. I guess you know I've been getting write-ups in the sports section of the *Times,* even in *Sporting World.* Max told me I'm a draw. People want to see me fight. Yeah, after I knocked out Flores, I'm now an attraction, Max said. He's working on a fight with Jimmy "Jumbo" Owens. Owens is a black guy. Max says he's a tough son of a gun and very popular. I've heard of him. Owens has had eighteen fights and never been KO'd." Nate stopped and took a breath.

"He's never been knocked out? Has he ever lost a fight?"

"One. He lost one by a decision."

"I don't quite understand. What does all this mean?"

"Honey, it means big money for me."

"No, I mean about Owens, the guy Max wants you to fight."

"It means he's only dropped one fight, and he was standing up at the end of that one. So was his opponent, but the judges voted for the other guy, not Jumbo."

"But, Nate."

"Listen up, sweetie. It means Max's going to pay me fifteen grand, win, lose, or draw. If I know Max, he'll bet on me and cut me in on some of his winnings."

"But, Nate, this will be only your fourth time in the ring. My God, Nate, anybody with brains would tell you this Jumbo's far more experienced than you. Oh, Nate, I'm afraid. Can't you see what I'm saying? You're meant for bigger and better things."

"Mist, fifteen grand in one evening is more than some poor saps earn all year. Max wouldn't throw me into a den of lions. He told me I'm ready for the big time. Look at it like this. Sometimes rookies in sports are so good they shine. They just stand out. That's how Max sees me. He wouldn't risk my neck, not for anything. You got to really know Max to get the picture."

"Look at yourself," she said. "Look at the man you are. I don't mean your body. I mean the total you. The real Nate Bradford."

"Uh huh. See, you're practically saying it right there. Look how I've come along. It takes more than raw strength. It takes brains too. I've got both the body and the mind. I can see myself being a real contender for the title. Maybe even the champ!"

"Nate, I know that getting into the ring with another man who's out to kill you if necessary is realistic. And I know every fighter needs to be confident or forget about being a prizefighter. But what if you've overestimated your ability? Do you know how dangerous that can make the situation?"

"But, Mist."

"Let me finish, honey."

Misty went on to tell Nate what a wonderful person he'd become. She said she knew he was brave, that he'd had terrible, tough times in his past and that things looked rosy now. But she said once again, "Just suppose you're making a mistake. A bad mistake."

Misty didn't wait for Nate to answer. She told him she realized how much respect Nate had for Max White. She accepted the fact Max looked after Nate above other fighters in his string of pugilists. She even admitted Max gave Nate more time and attention. He wouldn't want to see his fighter get hurt.

"Suppose he's wrong? Nate, ask yourself: is fighting a sport? Isn't the objective of any fighter to batter his opponent until the opponent collapses? Suppose you're the fighter that gets battered? What then, Nate? What'll you do then?"

Misty couldn't stop talking.

"Honey, the other day you said something about your future, what you could do as a career if you weren't a successful fighter. You said you might want to get a teacher's degree and be a physical education teacher. Why not pursue that course with the money you've earned?"

"But, Misty, this fight would only be a six-rounder, eighteen minutes in the ring. Do the math. I did. That's eight hundred and thirty-three dollars a minute. Who else makes that kind of money?"

Misty countered as she told him he needed to do the math. She pointed out all the hours of training required to earn that money.

Nate came around to making a promise that with God as a witness, he'd think seriously about all she had said. He told her they'd have another heart-to-heart talk but added, "After this match. I need this match."

She countered by saying she needed Nate. He was her guy. He had captured her heart and she wanted Nate's heart to keep beating.

"I couldn't bear the thought of your not coming to my apartment if you're … if you were killed or badly injured."

"God, Misty, I'm not going off to war somewhere!"

"Oh, it's easy for you to say that when you're in one piece. That's how I want you to stay, in one piece. Can't you see that? The first fight you had, remember that night? I walked by the arena and I saw a man begging. He was blind. He had a sign on him that read, 'Blind Ex-Fighter.' He was blind from fighting. Blind, Nate."

"Baby, let's finish our dessert and enjoy the rest of the evening. You know if you were in the audience for this fight, you'd bring me luck. I just know. I'll be okay. I will."

Misty insisted she couldn't bear to watch Nate fight.

Nate had an idea. She should come to the fight, but she should sit in the very last row. If she became upset, he told her she could walk around and ease the tension. He even suggested she get a hot dog and a soda, anything as long as she was there for him.

"We can be together right after I take this guy out."

Misty switched the conversation. She told him she was going to speak with her dad about his winery and the possibility that Nate could go to work for her dad. She pointed out that Nate could still go to school while he worked for him.

"That could be our future. I've always dreamed about going back to the community I came from, where I was born and raised, where I could work."

"At the winery?"

"Oh, no. As a head librarian. Somewhere not too far from Dad's winery."

"The other day you used the word *us*. I hope it's still us."

"You know it is, Nate. I love you so much. Can't you see that?"

She reached across the table, held both his hands, and prayed. "Lord God, protect this man, my Nate. Look after him in the days to come, and at the same time, protect his opponent. Forgive them both for their way of earning a living. Let them both see the light, your light, heavenly Father. Let them understand the horror of what they both do. Amen."

Fighting back tears, Nate said, "Let's finish now and go for that boat ride on the canal."

# CHAPTER TWENTY-THREE

The first thing Monday morning, Nate looked around for Max. "Have you inked the contract for my next fight?"

"Yeah, kid. Well, I got it here. It'll be goin' in the mail to Owens's manager this afternoon. Somethin' botherin' ya'? Somethin' on your mind? Anybody been botherin' with you, messin' with your mind?"

"Jeez, Max, why all the questions? Misty and I've been talking about this Jumbo guy, that's all. He's got six times more fights under his belt than I've got. She's worried, Max."

"Sounds to me like you're worried too. Hey, that's good, kid. No need to be so cock sure of yourself that you set yourself up to get beat. I'm glad she's got the jitters. I've given lots of thought to your fight. I'm positive you can take 'em. You're a talented kid. Remember the movie *The Natural?* Well, that's you, only you're a fighter, not a baseball player. You can play ball like *The Natural,* slug a guy like he creamed a baseball. I'll bet you could've been a jim-dandy ballplayer too, come to think of it. I'm sure if you get yourself into even better shape than you're now, it'll work. You'll win and you won't get hurt. You know the risks. You'll probably get some bumps. Can't help that. Every pug gets knocked around. That's the name of the game."

"Yeah, but I don't want to get beat to a pulp either, Max."

"Hell, kid. I got hurt plenty, but I survived. Look at me. I'm standin' right here, talkin' to you."

Nate protested mildly, but Max kept on with the pep talk. He told Nate to remember that he was Nate's manager and trainer. He promised Nate he'd throw in the towel to end the fight if he thought Nate was getting beat up. Then he mellowed somewhat and said he'd do what Nate wanted. He offered to take things slower.

"But remember, Nate. Some big bucks are gonna come our way. Hey, kid, if you make a buck, I make a buck. You'll make more than me. Lots of bucks. I got the feelin', kid. I got the feelin'."

He told Nate to do more of everything while

he trained. He said Nate should actually add five minutes more every time he jumped the rope, every time he punched the bag, every time he jogged. He ended by telling Nate that he hadn't fought cream puffs in his first three fights.

"They could fight. But so did you. And you won, kid. You won."

For the next three weeks, Nate did what Max told him to. Nate researched diets at the library. He filled his meals with protein. His body took shape without becoming muscle bound.

At the gym, Max called Nate into his office.

"Remember a picture I took of you when you first waltzed into my gym? I'm gonna get it now and show it to you."

Max went to a file drawer and pulled out a folder. Then he got out his Polaroid camera and snapped a picture of Nate in his boxing trunks. In a minute, he handed it to Nate and said, "Look at you. Are you the same guy? Heck no, kid! Heck no!"

The picture confirmed what Nate felt, what Max said. The guy in the original picture was a far cry from the new Nate. His thoughts took him back to the fellow on a path of destruction, living on the streets with a wine bottle in his hand.

Nate credited his haven of relief, the rescue mission, and the dedicated counselors who worked with him, Captain Swain in particular.

Nate returned to his workout routine.

# CHAPTER TWENTY-FOUR

Owens's manager inked the contract for Nate to fight his man, Jimmy "Jumbo" Owens. While Nate was doing warm-up exercises, Max approached him, waving the contract through the air. "I got it back, kid. The fight's on. You got a month to get ready to kick his butt. Fifteen big ones, kid! Fifteen big ones!"

"I guess that's good, huh, Max?"

"Whaddya mean, you guess that's good? It's great. You're movin' up, kid. Start thinkin' right. Start thinkin' you can handle this bozo. You gotta believe in yourself. Got me? "

"Yeah, yeah, sure, Max. Sure. I can take him. You really think I can, don't you?"

JOEY CHISESI AND DIANE CHISESI

"Jeez, kid. Stop talkin' that way. Yep. I know you can. You got to know it too, kid. Hear me? Get to work. You know what you got to do. Do it. The better your shape, the better your mind."

It was the first time Max lectured Nate in that tone of voice other than during a fight. Nate tried to tell himself Max was right. He knew what he had to do.

Nate was going to pick up a used car but decided against it. Walking and jogging would be better for him. After a rigorous workout at the gym, he called the car agency and canceled his meeting with a car salesman. Nate dropped by the library and asked Misty to take a break for a few minutes.

They found an empty table. There, Nate told her the fight was on. Misty turned a bit pale and said, "Oh, God, Nate. I was hoping you had changed your mind. Can you still get out of doing this?"

"Look, Misty, this can be my last fight. I promised you I'd think seriously about giving the fight game up, and I will. I'll really think on it, honest. See, with this kind of money, I can plan to do something like go to college, shoot for something good. I need you on my side now. Just for another month, one more fight. Please, Misty. Hang in there with me. Max said—"

"Oh, I know what Max said. He's not the one getting beat up fighting. You're the one."

Nate appeared shocked by Misty's retort. "Come on, honey. You're not upset with me, are you?"

"Yes, yes. I mean, no. I'm, I'm just scared."

"I need you, Misty."

"I need you too. That's the whole problem."

Finally, Misty added, "I need to get back to my desk, Nate. Come over tonight. Please?"

"You bet, Misty. See you later."

When they were together in her apartment, a very reluctant Misty promised to come to Nate's fight with Owens. Later that night, Nate walked to his apartment feeling that winning over Misty was as important as winning over Owens.

## CHAPTER TWENTY-FIVE

isty lived up to her promise. On Nate's big fight night, she came to the arena and found her seat in the next to last row, about as far from the ring as possible. In her purse she tucked extra handkerchiefs. She knew she'd be crying, terrified, worried about her guy.

Nate's bout with Owens would be the fifth bout of the evening, the semifinal fight on the Friday night fight card, one below the main event. Misty was reading the program when to her horror she noticed that Nate's fight would be a six-rounder. Had she heard wrong? Didn't Nate say the fight would be the usual four rounds? Could Nate have held this back from her in an attempt to spare her from worrying the past few weeks?

The fight before Nate's was in progress. Misty put the program card on her seat and went to the ladies' room; then she went to the refreshment counter and bought a soft drink. Nate had told her to walk around if she was nervous. Nervous? She thought she'd faint any moment.

She heard the bell sound for the final round before Nate's battle. Trying not to focus on the gladiators, she glanced at a woman seated beside her. The woman smiled and said, "You don't look like you belong here. My husband, Tom, loves the fights and drags me along. I'm getting to be an expert. The only thing I can't do is figure out who to bet on before the fights start. But I can tell you who won each fight, even before the ring announcer says his name."

Misty managed to say, "Do you have a feeling about this next fight?"

"Why? Are you betting this fight?"

"Oh, no, no. I never gamble. My boyfriend is Nate Bradford. He's fighting Jumbo Owens."

"This should be a good one. Jumbo's tough. He's a rugged guy. I hear Bradford's no pushover either. Your guy's a good looker from his picture in the paper. I can see why he's your boyfriend."

"Oh, there's a lot more to Nate than just being a good-looking man."

Just then the ring announcer called out, "The judges and the referee unanimously declare this fight no decision. A draw."

Loud boos filled the arena along with the stamping of feet.

Betters had the option of picking a winner or betting the fight a draw.

In a few minutes, Jimmy "Jumbo" Owens walked down the aisle, followed by his handlers. Owens wore a blazing red satin robe. Loud cheers greeted his entrance, an obvious favorite.

He climbed through the ring ropes. His trainer removed the red robe. Owens looked massive, with bulging arm and chest muscles. He began to loosen up near his corner, hitting at imaginary targets with his fists.

In what seemed like an eternity to Misty, Nate came down another long aisle. He too received cheers from fight fans who were following his progress as a young ring battler.

The woman next to Misty poked her. "He's a good looker, all right. I snapped his picture as he walked by. Wanna see it?"

"Oh, sure." Misty's hands trembled as she looked at the picture on the phone.

"Honey, relax. What's the worst that can happen? If he gets beat up, you can nurse him. I can think of lousier things to do."

Totally shocked by the words, Misty handed the phone back.

"I didn't want to come tonight. But I promised Nate I would to give him support."

"I think he saw you. Didn't you see him wave toward here?"

The ring announcer began his introductions. "This is the semifinal bout of the evening. Refereeing tonight's fight will be ex-light heavyweight champion, Jack Jamison. In the corner to my right and weighing in at a hundred eighty-six pounds, hailing from Seattle, Washington, is the promising light heavyweight, Nate "The Wanderer" Bradford.

Again, cheers rang out.

Misty said, "I can't stand it when they call him that." She said it loud enough to be heard by others seated near her.

"Calm down, honey. Calm down. It's just a name."

"And in the opposite corner to my left and hailing from Jersey City, New Jersey, is the winner of eighteen out of his nineteen fights, power-punching, hard-hitting, Jimmy "Jumbo" Owens."

Cheers and loud applause followed.

Referee Jamison motioned them to the middle of the ring for instructions. He warned them about low blows, hitting behind the head, and butting with their heads.

Bradford and Owens returned to their corners.

Max stood alongside Nate and held up his hands as targets for Nate's punches.

A buzzer sounded, and the fighters' assistants cleared the ring.

Ten seconds later, the bell rang for the start of the first round.

Misty looped her purse over her shoulder as she clutched the arm rests at her seat.

The gal next to her said, "Honey, he's a big boy. Relax before you have a heart attack."

"But I'm scared."

"Won't do any good for you to be scared. The guys in the ring ought to be scared."

Without comment, Misty got up from her seat and went to the ladies' room again.

• • •

Both fighters danced around the ring, feeling out each other like the start of a fencing match. Toward the end of the first round, Nate and Owens traded solid punches to the midsection.

The bell sounded, ending round one.

In his corner, Max wiped down a perspiring Nate. Max said, "Okay, kid, that was an even round. Feel those stomach punches?"

""Oh man, yeah. Yeah, I felt them. He had to feel mine too."

"Well, protect your gut, but watch your face too.

Keep movin'. Dance around him and look for shots. Counter punch. Counter punch. Got me?

"Yeah, I got you."

The warning buzzer sounded. Max jammed Nate's mouthpiece back into his mouth, slapped Nate in the face, and said, "Be ready."

The bell rang for round two.

Nate continued to dance around Owens. He tied up Owens whenever he could so the referee had to separate the two fighters and he told them both to fight. "Quit waltzing. Dog gone it. Fight."

Nate took a sharp left to his face and fended a right cross aimed at his midsection. But he grimaced from the stinging left jab. Nate fought back and caught Owens with a heavy blow to his middle. The battle was heating up.

The bell sounded for the end of round two.

Nate's face was red now. More sweat poured from his body.

Max threw a cold, wet towel at Nate and vigorously rubbed Nate's face.

Cut man Bernie massaged Nate's shoulders. Max did the talking.

"You got through another round, kid. You're even on my score card. Crank it up. You got as much wind as he got. You're as tough as he is. Crank it up." He pushed Nate's mouthpiece into place.

The warning buzzer came, followed by the bell for round three.

Max pulled the stool from under Nate and pushed him forward.

. . .

"Only four more rounds, young lady," the woman told Misty. Misty's eyes remained closed. The woman patted Misty on the arm and repeated, "Relax. Neither of those guys are taking a real beating so far. I got this fight even to now."

Misty turned to the woman. "I don't care who wins. I just want this over with."

"Come on now. You wouldn't want your guy to know what you just said, would you? Whose side are you on anyway? See Danny next to me? He played a lot of hockey. Got himself hurt a number of times. But I rooted for him."

An anxious Misty said, "Oh, you know what I mean. I just want this over."

. . .

The pace of the fight intensified. Both fighters pummeled each other. Nate had slackened his dancing around Owens. A quick left to Nate's face and a wicked right to his midsection dropped Nate to the canvas.

Nate fell near his corner. The referee began to count. "One, two."

Nate got to one knee, looked at Max as Max shouted, "Stay down. Let him count to eight. Get your bearings."

Referee Jamison counted to eight, and Nate got back on his feet.

He charged Owens, smashing him in the mid-section and then followed with his own right cross that saw Owens covering for protection. Nate had him against the ring ropes as the bell sounded, ending the third round.

Max squeezed the contents of a sponge onto Nate's face as Nate sank onto his stool in the corner. He spit out his mouthpiece into a water bucket.

Max shouted at Nate, "You okay? You okay? What round is this? Where are you?"

Breathing hard, Nate said, "I'm fine. I'm okay. Man, that guy can hit. I never saw that coming."

"That's the Nate I wanna hear from. Take a whiff of this."

Bernie rolled smelling salts in front of Nate's nose. Nate jerked his head.

Max said, "Three more to go. Can you hang in?

"I ain't gonna go three more."

"Whaddya mean, kid?"

"Just what I said."

• • •

Misty had left her seat. She walked up and down the corridor near the refreshment stand. The woman who had befriended her followed after her. "Your guy's all right. Didn't you see him go after the other guy? He's going to be a great fighter. He isn't hurt. I seen Danny get hit with a hockey stick. He got all stitched up, but he turned out okay. We been married all these years since, and you'd never know he got beat up on the ice."

The woman held Misty's hand and walked with her.

. . .

In the ring, Nate took deep breaths of air as Max fanned him with a towel.

"Round four. Two to go. You had him. You're just a little behind on my card. But be careful. You got a bit of a cut over your eye, but it's high up. The ref didn't bother to look at it. Okay, now go get 'em."

The warning buzzer sounded. In ten seconds, the bell rang for the start of round four.

Nate got up and pushed his way from his corner ropes. He charged into Owens. The two battlers stood toe-to-toe, slugging at each other. Nate took another right to the side of his head and slipped to the canvas, but he got right back up. Like a mad dog attacking another dog, Nate plowed punch after punch into Owens's midsection. He took punches from Owens in return, but he continued his surge until Nate landed rights and lefts to Owens's face.

Blood poured from Owens's nose. His mouth-piece flew from his mouth and out of the ring. But Owens remained on his feet. Finally, Nate caught Owens with a punch so devastating that Owens fell against the ropes as Nate hit him again and again.

Owens sank to the floor. The referee began his count, but a white towel flew out from Owens's corner. The fight was over.

Max and Bernie leaped to Nate's side. Nate himself was in a daze. They walked him to his corner and raised his arm in the victory sign. An exhausted Nate slumped to his corner stool.

Owens's handlers helped Owens to his feet. They threw water onto his face. Owens berated them. Ringsiders heard Owens shout, "Why'd you throw in the towel? Who's side you on anyway? Who's side you on? Nobody throws in a towel on me."

Owen's trainer shouted back at him, "Jumbo, you nuts? He was gonna beat you to a pulp. The referee wouldn't have let the fight go on. That kid's crazy."

Another of his handlers yelled at Owens. "Sit down and shut up. It's only the first time you been beat. You want to fight him another time? Okay. Just sit down and shut up."

. . .

Misty, devastated, thanked the woman. "Is it over?"

"Yeah. Your guy won. Didn't you see what happened?"

"Oh, thank God. Thank God. I've got to get down there to his dressing room."

"You can't go in there, but you can wait outside near the door."

The woman kissed Misty on her cheek.

. . .

Max continued to rub Nate's face while Bernie applied ice and an antibiotic cream to the cut above Nate's right eye.

The referee called for the microphone to be lowered, reached for it, and began his announcement. "Ladies and gentlemen, the winner on a technical knockout in the fourth round and still undefeated: Nate 'The Wanderer' Bradford."

Max pulled Nate up and raised Nate's arm high into the air. Max looked at the referee and shouted, "Technical knockout! Whaddya mean, technical knockout?"

The referee grinned at Max and turned his back toward Owens's corner.

Owens's face was a mess. Nate didn't appear to be a beauty queen either.

"Okay, kid. You can make it to the dressing room, can't you? Let's not look bad. Look like a winner."

Max threw Nate's robe around him, opened up the ropes, and Nate managed his way down the ring stairs.

Nate walked ahead of Max and Bernie.

Nate glanced around, looking for Misty, but he didn't see her. Applause greeted him as he headed past the rows of spectators.

Seated now on the dressing room table, Max cut the tape off Nate's gloves and pulled them loose.

"What did I tell you, kid? I knew you could take out this guy. Kid … Nate … you okay?"

"Yeah, yeah I'm okay. I won, didn't I?"

"You won. You had us worried, though, a couple times. Look, get your trunks off and get in the shower. It'll do you good."

Max saw Nate fall to his knees in the shower room.

# CHAPTER TWENTY-SIX

Misty's cell phone rang. "Hello, Dad," she said.

"How'd you know it was me?"

"Caller ID."

"Oh, that's right," Byron Wakefield said. "The world's getting too slick, too modern for me. How are you, sweetie?"

"I couldn't be healthier or happier, Dad. How are you?"

"Just a bit tired. It's hard to believe how the winery bookings have increased. We're busy, busy, busy!"

"That's good, isn't it, Dad?"

"Well, yes, but it sure keeps us hoppin'. Oscar

and I are sort of strugglin' with it all. Had to put another chap on the payroll. He helps, but bookin' all the events takes a lot of time. You know, honey, showin' the place to people who might want to rent the place, all of those things. Takes time, lots of time. When harvest time comes around, I'll be busier than a one-armed bandit in Vegas."

Byron told Misty how his event bookings doubled in recent weeks, including visitors to the Wakefield Vineyard and Winery. He explained how they gave away a free glass of wine with crackers and cheese to every visitor. He'd arranged for a couple college girls to cut up the cheese and handout the wine samplers.

"I have to make sure the gals are over twenty-one and that they don't serve wine to anyone who's tipsy. Can't afford any accidents stemmin' from here, ya know. Can't afford that."

"Dad, since when are you serving cheese and crackers with the wine? Is that something new?"

"Been doin' it for a while. Everybody comes here buys a bottle."

"A bottle of cheese?"

"No, no, a bottle of wine. Most often, a case of wine."

"Are you selling cheese too?"

"Yep, wine and cheese. They go together. We started selling cheese about six months ago. Didn't I tell you that? People love both. You know there's been a wine craze over the last decade. Haven't you noticed that out there?"

"No, Dad. This is a hard liquor town. It's been a Frank Sinatra/Dean Martin-type city for some time."

"Well, Northern California is wine country, believe me, honey."

Misty switched the subject. "How's your blood pressure, Dad?"

"I been watchin' it go up."

"Oh, Dad, have you been to the doctor lately?"

"I'm just jokin', Misty. I check it at the grocery store every couple weeks."

"I worry about you, Dad. Maybe I should come home and check on you."

Byron insisted he was okay. "You know what? Your fella, Nate, the boxer guy. What's he doin' besides gettin' a facelift?"

"Dad, that's not nice."

"Neither's his gettin' punchy, honey. Aw, I'm just kiddin' around, babe. I watch a lot of fights on the tube. Got me a big screen. I wonder how those dudes handle all the punches they get tossed at 'em."

Misty said she worried about Nate too. "I care for him very much."

"Figured so! That's one of the reasons I called ya. How'd he like to come out here and look things over?"

"Look things over? What does that mean?"

Byron reminded Misty about all the good things she'd told him about Nate in her letters. Then he told her that he needed a bright chap to work with him. In Nate's case, he explained, he'd be able to give up prizefighting. Maybe Misty could dangle the idea in front of Nate.

"You know, Dad, I've had the same thought. Of course, I have no right to interfere with your business."

"No, no, it's okay. Really. It's okay. He knows about the winery, doesn't he?"

"Yes, I've even given him books to read on the subject. You know about his background a bit from what I've told you. I might be concerned about the wine situation, but I'm positive he's beyond all that now."

"Well, honey, suggest he might want to come visit me out here. But don't tell him it's about a job. How about a position? How does position sound?"

"It sounds great. I just have a hunch it may sound good to Nate too."

Misty told her dad that Nate was grounded, unable to enter the ring for sixty days because of his injury from his fight with Owens.

"Boy, that sounds like he won the battle but lost the war. Is he still as bright and sharp as you claim?"

"Of course. Even more so."

"Well, I trust your judgment. Can you try and nail this down?"

Misty said she'd be with Nate that evening. She'd talk up a trip to Sacramento and the winery at Newcastle.

"Ah, that's a good daughter. Your mom would have been very proud of you. She's probably lookin' down at you at this very moment."

"Now, don't make me cry. Oh, before I forget, are you still wearing boots out there?"

"Now, what in the world brought that on, Misty? What's boots got to do with anything?"

"They're heavy, Dad. Wouldn't you be better off wearing sneakers or walking shoes? Boots are tiring."

"How'd I kill rattlers with sneakers?"

"Rattlesnakes? I thought boots were for killing cockroaches, you know, getting them into corners."

"I think we're both bein' silly now. Got to hang up. Give me a buzz as soon as you know something. Okay? Love you, Misty."

Misty touched end on her cell phone, poured soup she'd been simmering into a cup, sat down, and began to worry about her dad. She said a prayer for him and asked God for help in persuading Nate to meet with him and view the winery's operation.

Evening came around. Misty drove to Nate's apartment to pick him up. The two were to attend a social gathering at a library staff member's home on the Las Vegas outskirts. When she got there, he was standing curbside pretending to hitch a ride. She laughed and passed him by. She stopped a few yards away. He ran toward her and jumped in the car.

"What's the big idea leaving me stranded and alone?"

"Oh, was that you? I saw some sharp-looking fellow standing there. This guy looked so sharp I didn't think it was you."

Nate was dressed in a navy blue sport shirt with a golf motif in sharp contrast to his gray slacks. He presented a handsome figure of an athlete with his dark brown hair and his deep-set hazel eyes.

"I could go for a guy like you. Got a name?"

"Oh, yeah, sure. I'm Natty Nate. Hey, that sounds good. Think I'll use that professionally. Natty Nate."

"You weren't Natty Nate a couple weeks ago. You were more Flatty Nate."

"What do you mean, Flatty Nate? I knocked him out, didn't I?"

Misty took the opportunity to tell Nate about her dad's phone call. "There's a gentleman in Northern California who's eager to meet you."

Nate came back with, "Another fight promoter? A Hollywood producer, maybe? Whoever wants me and my life's story will have to pay plenty for it."

"Nate, you're acting silly. No, the man is my dad. He'd like you to come out to Newcastle, California, and see the operation. I believe he may have a position for you. The most violent part of it would be stomping barefoot on grapes. The worse that could happen would be to see your feet turn red and purple instead of your face."

"Ouch. That's a low blow. A referee would charge you with a foul. Besides, I look great with a red and purple complexion."

"You think so? Seriously, Dad would like you to fly out and see his vineyard and winery. He's probably in denial, but he's been having some blood pressure problems, and I'm concerned. He needs a top assistant. He's got a man who's been with him a long time, but he needs a younger fellow. Dad's interested in you."

"You mean give up my profession? Mist, I'm just getting started. Max says I got the potential to be a top-notch fighter. Who's gonna stand in my way? All the fighters in my weight class are bums, real bums."

"Oh, Nate, you've got to stop fooling yourself. All right. Let's say you've got potential. Does that mean getting beat up every couple months for a few dollars?"

"But, Mist, I'm Nate. I'm just beginning to realize who I really am."

"Honey, you could be a dead guy. People would forget you in a few days. Can't you see the horror of the fight game? Can't you see how worried we were when they took you to the hospital after your fight with Owens? You looked terrible. We were scared out of our wits."

Misty explained how she shouldn't dictate his future. She used the illustration of looking into a crystal ball, but she found no answer in it. Misty told him that a position with her dad wouldn't have the same excitement he found in boxing, nor perhaps the earnings Nate could accumulate, but then she said something she hoped really hit home.

"Nate, think about a bright future in a growing business, a future for us."

"*Us?* You used that word once before. You mean that?"

"Yes, yes, I do mean that. I love you so much."

Thoughts raced through Nate's mind. He almost mumbled out loud, "What did I have to lose? After all, I'm on the shelf for a while until I heal. Maybe I should look into this invitation. I'm really lucky. Misty's so sincere."

Nate paused for a few moments. Then he said, "Misty, you got a deal. I'll meet with your dad."

They pulled to a stop near the home of her friend. "I'll call Dad in the morning. Oh, thank you, Nate. Thank you."

The party became a joy-filled event for the two of them. It lasted until almost midnight. They drove back to Nate's apartment. They could barely find the willpower to release their embrace. Nate kissed her good night one more time.

# CHAPTER TWENTY-SEVEN

The next morning, Misty called her dad and told him she'd talked with Nate and he was agreeable to visiting the winery. "He seemed really sincere, Dad."

Byron told Misty he was pleased. "What would you like me to do?"

"Get him booked on a flight and make it as soon as you can. The sooner, the better. He's not tied down to anything right now, Dad."

"Give me an hour or so and I'll call you back. Okay, sugar?"

"Okay, Dad, an hour. Thanks."

# CHAPTER TWENTY-EIGHT

As Nate stepped off the plane in Sacramento, he felt the same lonely feeling he'd fostered for so many years of his life.

His plan was to visit the Wakefield Vineyard and Winery by himself, no influence from Misty. No prodding from her either.

Nate found his luggage that Misty loaned him and then spotted Byron on the walkway outside the baggage area. He recognized Byron Wakefield from pictures Misty had shown him before he left her in Las Vegas. He saw a tanned and well fit man in his late fifties.

They greeted and headed for the airport parking area where Byron had parked his pickup truck.

Nate tossed his luggage in the rear of the truck, and as the two of them headed out of the airport, he said, "Well, I'm anxious to hear about the Wakefield Vineyard and Winery and its operation."

"Honest, Nate, nothing as exciting as prize-fighting. You know the expression. It's like sitting around and watching grass grow. Of course, I'm exaggerating. There's a heck of a lot to do and a lot to worry about."

"Misty didn't tell me much about the worry part. She did say you've got your hands full. She said you have some fifty acres you operate. Right?"

"Yep," Byron said. "It's a pretty good-sized spread. We grow the vines that produce the grapes and bottle the product right there. We also have all kinds of affairs—private birthday parties, wedding receptions, club dinners, all kinds. Actually, we're always busy, particularly on Friday and Saturday nights. Lots of Sunday afternoon events too."

"I wasn't aware of all that, Mr. Wakefield. Misty kind of left that out of my schooling."

"Hey, no need for this Mr. Wakefield stuff. Byron, or just plain By is plenty good enough. And how's my daughter? How's Misty?"

"She's fine. Great. You have a wonderful daughter."

"I think so too. I often think how much Misty's mom would have wanted to be with her daughter.

I'm sure Misty told you she died a few days after Misty came into this world."

"Yes, sir, she did. Your wife developed an infection in the kidneys, right?"

"That's right. Docs did everything they could. No luck. It just wasn't meant to be."

Byron reached the main road, Interstate 80, and headed eastward in the direction of Reno, Nevada. Finally, he spoke again.

"Reno is about a two-hour drive from Newcastle. You know about Reno? Can't compare Reno to Vegas. Both places drain your money. In Vegas, you lose your dough with all the glitz and glamour. In Reno, you just plain lose your dough, if you catch my drift," Byron said.

"I had a bit of luck in Vegas," Nate said. "Actually, it turned my life upside down, but for the good, if that makes sense."

"Young man, you're one of the very few that can make that statement."

"It did. I guess I was lucky, real lucky. If I hadn't had that luck, I wouldn't have found your daughter. That was real luck."

"Misty told me a little about that. She feels fortunate too."

As they continued the drive eastward on I-80, Byron explained where they were. He told Nate how they could reach another wine-growing area, Napa, California, by driving in the opposite direction. Byron explained Napa was west from where they were; they could reach the Napa-Sonoma wine country on the way to the ocean.

"I've seen that name, Napa, before. In fact, when Misty told me you owned a vineyard and winery, I figured it was in Napa. Do you grow the same kind of grapes at your place in Newcastle?"

"Good question. No, we grow different kinds of grapes. We grow Zinfandel grapes. Napa grows white wines. Sounds like Misty prepped you a bit. Right?"

"Heck, Byron, I know a little bit about wine, especially how to consume it. That's a part of my life I'd like to wipe out forever."

Nate continued asking questions about Napa and Newcastle. Byron told him they were about a hundred miles apart. He explained how the soil in Napa was richer due to more moisture in the air.

"Comes up from the ocean. The ocean's not far from Napa. They get cooler nights and mornings year round. My soil is decompressed granite. My grapes need to be drought resistant. My drainage is better for Zinfandel growing. In fact, that's part of the worry factor."

"The worry factor?"

"Oh, yeah. Couple of seasons ago, I lost well over half my crop. It's not supposed to rain in July in the Sierra foothills area, but it rained like heck. I took a pasting. Guess that's the nature of being a farmer. Growing grapes and harvesting them is agriculture, like a farmer with the same risks."

Nate was impressed with Byron.

"Got to be honest about weather in Newcastle. The winters have a number of damp and dreary days."

Nate said, "I was raised on that stuff in Seattle. Talk about dreariness. We'd go days at a time without seeing the sun."

They continued talking as Byron swung his truck onto Highway 65, now only fifteen miles or so from Newcastle.

As they drove, Byron continued to fill in Nate on the growth taking place in the communities around his winery. Byron pointed out the Thunder Valley Casino, right by Lincoln. He added that people didn't have to go to Reno now to lose their money. They could easily do this right in their own backyard.

"I understand that casino takes in more money than any other in the state. I go there once in a while, not to gamble but to eat. See that tower over there? That's a new addition to the casino. There's gonna be a hotel and a theater for big shows when it's finished. Lots of new parking too. People in Lincoln were worried when the casino got built, concerned about crime. But crime didn't increase a bit. Lots of people from Lincoln go there."

They passed through the burgeoning town of Lincoln and headed east on Road 193.

"You sure know your way around."

"Ought to. Lived here a long time. I've seen all of this expansion. Seen it from the ground up."

"What's out here, the Newcastle area, I mean?"

Byron gave him a verbal cook's tour, describing all the services, stores, and recreational activities.

"All this stuff is just a few minutes from Newcastle. As for food shopping, we got major stores all over the place.

"What's your population around here?" Nate asked.

"Add all the towns together and it's reached about two hundred fifty thousand. Biggest problem is traffic. It crawls on Highway 65 and Interstate 80 most every day. Getting through it can be a can of worms. I think the planners overlooked this problem. But there's gonna be a bypass on Highway 65. It's started already." Byron chuckled. "Best way is don't get on the roads during peak traffic hours. Works for me."

"Boy, you'd have made a great tour guide," Nate said.

"Naw, I'm a grape grower and winemaker." Byron said he knew Nate was used to a different world, at least for the last few months. He joked about Nate getting his handsome face relocated.

Nate laughed and then asked Byron what he meant by that.

"I watch fights on TV. I shudder when fighters get plastered in the puss. Besides, you can use some serenity."

"Maybe I can. Maybe it's about time I do."

The two of them were now on the last leg of their trip to the Wakefield Winery.

# CHAPTER TWENTY-NINE

"My little town of Newcastle has about a thousand people. Doubt if it gets any bigger. We're in Placer County, to be specific. Placer County got named from the gold mining process they used in this area. Ever hear of that, Nate?"

"Yeah, I learned about that from a chemistry teacher in high school. It's where you wash away material you've scooped out of the water and hope what's left in your pan is gold."

"Good answer," Byron said. "Shows you were listening to your teacher."

"Well, once in a while anyway." Nate grinned.

"Here's the last stretch. Beautiful country, ain't

it? So peaceful in these Sierra foothills. This is all part of the Sacramento Valley. Driving tour ends here. What do ya think of the view now?"

"Man, it's awesome."

They approached the top of a hill on a narrow, asphalt-paved road. At the crest, Byron brought the truck to a stop.

"Step out, Nate. Look at 'er from here. All that's missing is a lake or an ocean down below. I sure love these here foothills. See the Sierras to the north-east? And look below at those vines. Let me tell ya, if order in your life is what you're lookin' for, then the way those beauties grow should give you all the order your life can handle."

Byron led Nate along rows of grapevines. He pointed out how the rows of vines faced south and southwest.

Nate noticed all the vines loaded with bunches and bunches of grapes.

"Come 'ere, Nate. See how every leaf is spaced the same distance between itself and the next leaf? Notice the same with the branches. That's the job of growing vines, the farmer's job, although Mother Nature has a lot to do with it too. Takes a lot of work to remove all the unwanted growth. With as many acres as I have, well, it's a huge job. That's where the helpers come in handy, to say the least."

"Wow. Each vine looks perfect, like a picture. Incredible, a thing of beauty."

"Yep. You know how order's needed in one's life? Well, it's the same growing grapes. Matter of fact, with growing anything in large numbers," Byron said.

"So the vines grow back each year, right? You don't plant new vines? Start from scratch?" Nate said.

"Nope. If something goes bad with a section of grapes, ya might have to, but assuming no disasters from disease or bad weather, the vines grow again each year."

"I learned a little bit about grape growing," Nate said.

"So the cycle works like this: Clear all the unwanted growth at the end of the grape harvesting. Cultivate the earth around the vines. Treat the soil with fertilizers and keep watch for fungus or insects. As the vines grow, clear out any extra growth that pops up. Pick the grapes at the end of the growing season or just before. When the grapes look ripe to your taste or color, it's time to pick 'em. From there, it's to the winery and the crushing. Bottling is next. That's an oversimplification, I know, but that's the program. Got all that?" Byron said.

"Wow. Is there a written test next?" Nate said, joking. "Oh, by the way, who buys the wine?"

"We got customers from years back. They like my wine. They're Zinfandel lovers. We grow and bottle hundreds of cases of Zinfandel. You'll find the Wakefield brand in stores on the West Coast in particular. We price it midrange. Not too cheap and not overly expensive."

Nate thought how Byron must be at peace with himself looking at his acreage and the picturesque landscape that stretched out in front of them. At once he understood the fondness Byron felt for his land and the growth on it. But then he asked himself, *Is it too calm?*

After a few seconds, Byron pointed left toward the top of another hill and said, "There's my house. Looks good, doesn't it? Not brand-new like some homes in Lincoln, but I've done a lot of work keeping it modern as possible. Wanted you to see this view first. We'll back up and go on down and then up to the house."

Byron maneuvered the truck around, found the main road, and headed to his house. As they approached a long driveway, Nate was struck by the beauty of some fifty Italian Cypress trees, twenty-five or so on each side of the driveway. They stood like guards protecting Byron's home.

"My God, Byron, this is a palatial entranceway. Holy smoke. I've never seen anything like this. It's like you'd see in a movie or a picture of a villa in Italy."

Byron grinned.

In a few more minutes, they were in the parking area. Nate noticed the neatness of the landscaping.

Purple flowers covered the ground. Red-, pink-, and peach-colored rose bushes blushed with blooms planted in proper arrangements. A maze of palm trees seemed to wave at them on another side of the house. The palm trees formed a natural barrier between Byron's home and the vineyard.

"What a yard you got here. There's an order to your ground designs. Did that idea come to you from your vineyard?"

"I suppose so," Byron said. "It's a hobby of mine. 'Course, some people think growing grapes is a hobby. Not so. It's lots of work and time. The grapes grow orderly. Why not have my flowers do the same? Got to admit I use workers to help in the garden area too."

"Where do you get all the helpers?"

"There's a junior college right near here. Get them from there. Heck, they're literally volunteers; you know, kids interested in horticulture and agriculture. Botany students and you name it."

"Really? Do they know what they're doing?"

"Not till I show 'em. Then they make good workers."

Byron went on to describe his top staff.

"Oscar's my top gun, Oscar Deering. Been with me for a lotta years. He's got a small home at the other end of the vineyard. Never got married. He's a good man. Never wanted a ton of responsibility, but handles things well. Between Oscar and me, well, we get things done right. Oscar helps me in the winery too when we host events. But he's not a kid anymore either. Here, grab your luggage, Nate."

Byron told Nate about some of his and Oscar's duties while he led Nate into his house.

"Let's go in and have a cold one. Got chilled Wakefield White Zinfandel. Got cold Miller in the bottle or soft stuff. You got a preference?"

"Yep. Soft stuff. Never drink on the job," Nate said.

"You're on the job already? You've hardly seen the joint! How do I know I can afford you?"

"Hey, you can afford me," Nate said, smiling.

"My daughter sure has confidence in you. I know she cares for you in a big way," Byron said, repeating what he had told Nate back at the airport.

"I always thought Misty had real class and a ton of good taste," Nate said, still grinning.

"Here's your soft drink. Enjoy. We'll take a tour of the winery in a while. Got plenty of time."

Byron had built his house to capture the depth of the vineyard along with the hills and vales. As the sun moved to the west, rows of symmetrically aligned grapes covered the dips in the land.

Clouds were a rarity at this time of the year, but a few wisps floated to the east in the distance, dancing in the pale blue sky.

Nate knew right away how this scene of serene

tranquility must capture Byron's heart over and over again, crop after crop, year after year.

Nate spoke up after a few seconds. "It's easy to see how good this is for you, how much this must mean to you."

"Yeah. Add up the profits from those grapes, plus the joy I get looking out at this sight, well, I guess you're right. You hit the nail on the head." Byron looked pensive. "Can't think of anywhere else I'd like to live. Well, maybe Sicily."

"Sicily," Nate said. "Why Sicily?"

"Well, look at it this way. From the pictures I've seen, they grow tons of grapes there. Olives too. Right on the side of the mountains. But that ain't all. At the base of those mountains, there's the Mediterranean. Ever see paintings of that scene? Got to be beauty beyond description. How about that? And you sit on balconies of villas and look at the view while ya drink a glass of red wine. I'll overlook the fact that it's red wine instead of my Zinfandel." Byron laughed. "Actually, we grow four varieties of Zinfandel."

Nate was studying Byron. He pretty well guessed Byron's age, probably in the late fifties. He knew too how comfortable he felt being with the father of the gal he cared for so much.

After a refreshing beverage, Byron, tanned but not wrinkled, grabbed a farmer's straw hat on the way out of the house.

Nate knew now where Misty inherited her beautiful and exciting eyes. Byron's eyes sparkled when he spoke of his vineyard. Nate had seen the same gentle kindness in Misty's eyes.

While flying from Las Vegas, Nate had thought about his future, his relationship with Misty, and his boxing career. He asked himself about the possibility he might wind up in a small California town. *But,* he told himself, *that could be good.* A few months ago he didn't have a future other than a place to flop with a bottle of wine.

Then he found Max, who helped restore his faith in people. And Misty. Well, Misty was the saint sent him to resuscitate his soul.

What about the dollar bill he'd found on the street in Vegas? Was there a story behind that single piece of green paper? He hadn't forgotten the role the rescue mission had played in his teetering life either. He'd been rescued by the strangest of circumstances. All those visits with Captain Swain. Heck, it was like having a psychiatrist or a personal psychologist for free. Captain Swain was even closer to him than doctors might have been, and the Captain had been exactly where he'd been, a bum, a lost soul.

Byron led the two of them into his jeep and drove on a path to the winery.

Nate's mind whirled through the memory of his alcoholic binges not long past. His yearning for cheap wine, wine strong enough to put him into la-la land raced through his mind. Could he resist this temptation?

"You probably saw the other building when we first drove in. It's near the house so I can keep an eye on everything. Guess I told you we hold all kinds of events there, plus the wine tasting tours that come through."

Nate remembered and told Byron so. Byron said, "Shows you're listening young fella'. Shows your listening."

Built on a plateau at the top of the hill stood an attractive building, river rock constructed, with a sign over the entrance, "The Wakefield Winery." The sign, modestly carved, carried the tradition of wineries, those that didn't boast of their existence but rather the caliber of their product.

Byron told Nate about the history of the rock construction and how the area was settled by Portuguese and Italian men. "They worked in rock quarries around the city of Rocklin, a few miles away. That's how Rocklin got named," he explained. "It took master workmen to build this, and I think it adds character and charm to my winery."

Nate heartily agreed. They entered the building. The coolness of the interior struck him right away. "Those rocks also absorb the heat, but they keep the inside temperature at a comfortable level, even though it's near ninety degrees outside. That's great grape growing temperature, but you can be quite comfortable inside," he said.

"This building's air conditioned and we have a special exhaust fan that draws the warm air out. Just one of the reasons our winery caters so many events. 'Course, the natural beauty of this place is the clincher. Guests fall madly in love with everything we offer. We have a couple exceptional caterers who we contract with. They bring in really good food. As you can see, we have a pleasant interior atmosphere here, even a dance floor that's as slick as a hound's tooth. Just another amenity we offer. Also got bands or DJs to bring in, and they do a great job. All in all, we've got one of the most popular and well-received facilities for miles around. Getting to be a real chore, however. I know I could turn down events, but I don't want to get that kind of reputation."

"Wow, you would never suspect a winery to be dealing with other things. I thought a winery was a winery."

"Well, now, did Misty tell you also that we're giving cheese bits and crackers to everyone who samples our wines? See the gal over there by that wine bar? I'll show you the cheesy aspect." Nate didn't have time to react before Byron said, "Ha, that's a joke, son. The last year we've been doin' the cheese thing, and it's payin' off. See, we get more per bottle sellin' wine from here than we get by the case to our distributor merchants—the stores and outlets that sell Wakefield wines.

"Look, there's a car comin' down the road. Watch how this works."

Nate was becoming more fascinated by the minute.

Four people got out of the car and entered the winery. They headed for the wine bar. Byron didn't recognize them as repeat customers, so he told Nate, "They're probably tourists and found out about us from the chamber of commerce. No doubt someone there told them about our wine and cheese thing and they thought they'd check it out for themselves."

Sure enough, the guests began sampling a glass of wine at one of the tables near the wine bar. Nate and Byron were too far away to pick up their conversation, but Byron said, "If they want, they can walk around the lower area, see how we make the wine, and even go out and see the vines for themselves."

In a few minutes they returned to the wine bar. Nate and Byron watched. One of the men reached into his wallet to pay for a couple bottles of Wakefield's finest. The hostess behind the bar pointed to a stairwell that led to the winery itself on the lower deck.

"See what I mean, Nate? If they were locals, they'd probably go sit on the balcony and gaze at our million-dollar view. That's how word gets around."

"So I see," Nate said.

"People talk about us. Assumin' they were from around here, they might want to hold a weddin' reception or some other special event in my building."

"Amazing. Just amazing."

"So you can tell why I need someone in addition to Oscar to run this show, and it's getting to be a show. You know about the old saying, never a dull moment? Well, there's never a dull moment here until nightfall, and only if we don't have something going on in the evening."

Byron then took Nate on a tour of the building. He showed him the kitchen, where the catered food was brought in and prepared, and then the rest of the building, particularly the winemaking area.

"See, everything starts from the start, so to speak. The vines grow, produce grapes, mature, get harvested, converted into wine, and bottled. Like I said before. To top all of this off, we've got all the events that take place. Oh, did I tell ya that every event includes a purchase of at least ten cases of wine? That's one hundred twenty bottles. I would make an exception if a religious group came here, but we've only had two of them in all the years we've been in operation."

"Wow. That's all I can say. I'm overwhelmed. Can I see the view from the balcony?"

"Sure. Come on out here."

The two of them left the main ballroom and walked to the balcony.

"Rest your bones, son. Gaze out on this scene. What do ya think?"

"Super. I think it's great. I'd call it awesome."

"Coming from a tough guy boxer, you wax poetic."

"My concern is the bookwork involved. Do you have to go to accounting school to hack that aspect of the business? And how about marketing?"

"Hey, if I can do it, you can do it. I'll be here to help. Ain't goin' nowhere, I'm not."

"That's right. I'm not replacing you, am I? I'd be an associate. Would that be the right word?"

"Someday, you could be the total hundred yards, the big cheese. You should pardon the expression, the jug of wine. Who knows?"

"You're not saying anyone can learn in a short time what it's taken you years to learn?"

"Son, with my tutelage, you can be a farmer in no time. Biggest ingredient in learnin' to do anything is desire. You gotta have will, the will to do somethin'. I hate to go back to your boxing situation, but I bet you had more will than skill for the first couple fights. Am I right?"

"Yes, you're right. But I had the muscle power to pull me through as well."

"Well, Nate, your muscles can be put to the

test out here too. They'll come in handy along with brain power."

Nate stayed on with Byron for the week. Three events took place at the winery: a wedding reception, a golden anniversary celebration, and a sixtieth birthday party. Byron let Nate be the guy in charge of all three. He stayed in the background while Nate fielded special requests and saw that things went without a hitch.

Nate recognized the alcoholic consumption hazard as the number one issue for him. But he enjoyed being a watchdog. Two were evening events, and one took place during the afternoon. Nate became aware that several times some girls flirted with him. He didn't want to offend anyone, but he clearly made known his position as "a guy in charge, period."

When it was time to leave Byron, he took Nate to the airport on a different route to show him more of the countryside.

At SAC International, Byron bid Nate a pleasant good-bye but added, "Young man, I feel in my bones a great future for the Wakefield Winery, for you, and for my daughter. Tell Misty you passed muster with flying colors. If you're too modest to tell her, I guarantee you I'll be telling her and soon. Oh, and, Nate, be sure you tell her I've been checking my blood pressure and I'm on blood pressure meds the doc gave me. Don't want her to worry about her ole man. Deal?

"Deal," Nate replied.

Byron reached for Nate's right hand and gave it a firm shake. "At least I can say I shook hands with a professional fighter, hopefully a retired fighter."

"Don't watch for me on TV out here, Byron. I doubt if I'd have of made it that big. Anyway, thanks for a great week. I'm so glad I got to know you. Misty couldn't have picked a better man to be her father."

"Don't think Misty had much choice," Byron said with a big grin. "Take care, Nate, and tell Misty hello from her ole man."

"You bet, Byron."

Nate picked up his luggage and headed into the airport.

# CHAPTER THIRTY

A shes floated around Max's feet as he walked outside the arena. Charred and brown, an empty layer of steel and ashes lay spread in front of him. Max stood stunned. He stared at the gaping hole between Gerald's Place and the building next door.

Although the arena was off the main drag, the effect of the fire had drawn an enormous amount of attention.

A reporter pounded on the back of a van, urging his partner to let him in. A frustrated cameraman fiddled with his gear and tugged on his camera strap. After a few minutes, he walked around what remained of the fight arena and snapped more pictures as the sun started to break the surface of the horizon.

Max watched the photographer. He considered talking to him to recover some of the film for posterity's sake but stopped himself. Thoughts whirled through his mind. He watched as the men from the fire department continued to soak the remains of the building. The sun now encased the firefighters while they worked. Max stood, anxious, in continuing disbelief.

He had received a call from the fire department during the early morning hours and arrived as fast as he could. Max had managed a quick call to Nate. Nate in turn phoned Misty. They agreed to meet at the site of the fire.

The fire department remained for many hours, part of the sprawling scene of police and fire trucks, camera crews, and photographers that filled the back street.

Max winced as a small plume of smoke whipped past. His eyes watered from a mixture of smoke and tears. A terrible look of concern covered his face. As he rubbed his eyes, he felt a light tap on his shoulder. He turned around and stepped back toward where Nate and Misty stood, grateful they had arrived. Max pointed to the remains of the arena but said nothing.

Later that day, when evening arrived, Max had a chance to stop and compose himself. Alone in his apartment, he poured a stiff drink and sat at his kitchen table. At least his gym, Gerald's Place, wasn't damaged. All the preventive water used to protect his gym would eventually dry off in the hot Vegas sun, but the arena damage would put him in debt.

Max finished off his drink and slammed the glass on the table. He'd have to wait for the fire and police departments to determine the cause of the fire.

But Max had suspicions of his own. He looked at the whiskey bottle sitting across from him and paused. If there ever was an occasion to finish a bottle off, it would be now.

Max had quit drinking years ago and never felt the temptation return until now. He'd kept himself busy in the boxing game, becoming instrumental in building the character of his boxers. They looked up to him. He couldn't let any of them down.

Angrily, Max stood up, grabbed the bottle from the table, capped it, and shoved it back into a cabinet. Crazed for a brief moment, he lit a cigarette and inhaled, letting the smoke curl out from his nose.

He heard a loud knock at his door. Surprised, he opened it and peered out.

"I thought you could use some company, Max," Nate said. "I was worried about you. Have you eaten yet?"

Max wiped his lips with his shirt sleeve as Nate walked by him into the apartment.

"What's up, Nate?"

"I'm gonna' crash on your couch, if you don't mind."

Max paused for a moment and then decided. "Yeah, that'd be fine. Make yourself comfortable. But ain't you supposed to be with your girlfriend?"

Nate told Max that Misty was at home. Then they got to talking about boxing, particularly about Max's past career in the sport.

The next morning, the phone rang in Max's apartment. An arson investigator from the downtown police station was on the line.

"Max, we're positive you lost the arena to arsonists. We found five hot spots. Those spots were started from the outside. There's a good chance your night guards didn't hear a thing. Whoever started this fire poured gasoline in five places and probably started the fires within moments of each other. We noticed some residue with a gasoline odor, as well as heavy burning at those spots. In plain English, the arsonists didn't care if we detected the way the fires were started, or they were just plain stupid to do it that way. I'd guess they wanted to burn you out of business. Get the picture?"

"Oh, yeah. I got the picture all right."

"Know anybody who wanted you hurt in some way?"

"Know anybody? Yeah, I know the guys."

"You do? Who are they? You know, crackpots

like this could have done more stupid things like torching your place with people in it. As it is, only the night watchmen were there, and luckily they got out. One of them told us that he saw the smoke come into the building in different places. Further confirms our theory, Max … Max, are you there?"

"I'm here all right, but I'm really ticked off. I know who did this, and I know why."

"You do, huh?"

"Yeah, I do!"

"Okay, Max, we'll be over in about an hour. Okay?"

"Okay. Sure."

Max hung up and said to Nate, "We got problems, kid. Real problems. But I'm gonna fix 'em. I don't want you involved in any way with the arson cops. Okay? I didn't want you to know about this. Some guys wanted you to throw the fight with Owens. I never got involved with dirty stuff like that. I sure as heck didn't want you involved either. You just keep this to yourself, got it? Understand? Now, grab some breakfast, kid, and then get out of here."

"Sure, Max. You positive you'll be okay by yourself?"

"Yeah, yeah, I can handle this myself."

After a quick breakfast, Nate said, "Well, I'm coming back over later today."

Max nodded as he looked at pictures of the fire in the morning newspaper.

# CHAPTER THIRTY-ONE

Continuing his anxiety over Max, Nate tried to call him a number of times in the early afternoon.

Nate walked over to Misty's apartment as soon as she returned from work.

"I think I'll call his apartment again, but I bet he's not there," Nate said. Sure enough, there was no answer. "Well, let's grab supper and hit the road. You know, I haven't got a clue where to look for him. You're more familiar with this town than I am."

"Not with that part of Max's world," Misty said. "With thousands of people on the streets, it'll be like finding a needle in a haystack."

"We'll just have to go into a few more joints. That's all I can think to do right now."

After they gulped down their supper, Misty changed into fresh clothes, and they got into her car.

Even though her apartment was a number of blocks from the main casino area, they decided to start at outlying casino bars to search for Max. But luck wasn't with them. No Max.

After a couple hours of unrewarded searching, they called it quits. Nate used Misty's cell phone to call to Max again, to no avail.

Finally, Nate said, "Can you come with me to his apartment? I know it's close to nine thirty, but I'm really worried about him. Maybe he doesn't want to talk to anybody on the phone right now. He can be a stubborn guy, you know."

Misty agreed. She drove as Nate gave directions to Max's apartment. In a few minutes, Misty pulled up to the apartment complex and found a parking spot. She touched the remote on her key ring to lock the doors.

Max's apartment was on the fourth floor. Nate reached into his pocket for the key Max had entrusted to him some months back, fitted it into the lock, and opened the door.

Suddenly, Misty let out a cry of horror. "Oh my God! Oh, no. Oh dear God!"

Max lay on the floor. Dried blood covered his

head and face. At the same time, Misty handed her cell phone to Nate. "Get help, Nate."

Nate dialed 911. "We need help right away. Apartment four twelve, fifteen seventeen Arroyo Boulevard. He's on the floor."

"Who's on the floor? Are you sure he's not breathing?"

"He's not breathing. I'm, I'm afraid he's dead. I think he's dead."

The dispatcher responded, "We're sending a rescue squad and the police right now. Do you know the identity of the victim?"

"Yes, it's Max White. He's the owner of the arena. It burned down last night. He runs Gerald's Place too. That's the gym next door to the arena … I mean where the arena used to be."

Already Nate could hear the wail of sirens.

As two emergency medical technicians entered Max's apartment, Nate pointed to his body. One EMT bent over Max's body and felt for a heart beat. Blood no longer streamed from his wound. His eyes were still open and vacant. Two uniformed policemen arrived.

"Better call the coroner in on this one," one medic said. One of the officers said, "My God, that's Max White. He's the fight promoter."

The other cop looked at Nate and Misty. "What happened here?"

"We don't know," Misty said. "We've been searching all over town for Max. The arena burned down last night, and we wanted to check on him, see if he was all right. We found him lying there, just as you see him now."

"How'd you get into his apartment?" the other officer said.

"I have a key," Nate said. "Max gave me a key a few weeks ago."

One of the EMTs interrupted. "I'd say he fell against the edge of this glass table. I think you'll find he'd been drinking."

An empty whiskey bottle sat on the table.

"But Max quit drinking a long time ago," Nate said.

"Hey, maybe he started again. The coroner's office will find out if and how much," the other technician replied.

Nate said, "First, the arena. Now, Max. Man, this is too much."

Two plainclothes detectives joined the police officers and EMTs now. The uniformed policemen looked at them and one said, "This is your case now, but I'd say this man died from a fall when his head hit the end of the table there."

The other said, "He's Max White. You know him. He's the fight guy."

One of the detectives said, "Who are these people?" He pointed to Nate and Misty.

"We're friends of Max," Misty said.

"I boxed for Max," Nate said, his voice quivering. "He was my manager. He gave me my first fight chance. We both loved Max."

"Sorry. By the way, I'm Detective Brent Gregory, and my partner here is Larry Davenport. You understand you'll both need to go downtown and make a complete statement."

"This is just a formality. You found his body and you're obviously the first ones on the scene. It's a formality. Understand?"

"We understand. It's just that, well, this is awful." Misty began to cry.

Davenport reached into his pocket and handed her a tissue. She put her head on Nate's shoulder, and he pulled her into his arms.

"I know, Misty, I know."

"We'd like to find out what happened before he fell. When this story makes the news, someone is bound to step forward and remember where he was the last few hours of his life," Davenport volunteered.

"And speaking of the media, here they are now," Gregory said as half a dozen news people stepped into Max's apartment.

Davenport stopped them short. "No pictures here, folks. Just give me a couple minutes, and I'll fill you all in on the details as we know them."

"Isn't the victim Max?" shouted one newsman. "He's the same guy that just had the arena destroyed. Right?"

"Yeah, yeah, that's him. No pictures, understand? No pictures of him this way."

With that, one of the EMTs returned with a canvas and covered Max White's body.

Detective Davenport turned to Nate and Misty and said, "You have your own car?"

Nate nodded.

"We have to make a thorough inspection of this apartment. Meanwhile, I'll need both your names and where we can reach you. My fingerprint guy'll be along any minute. When he's through, we'll meet you back at precinct headquarters. Know where it is?"

Misty nodded.

"Good."

"Coroner's here," Gregory said from the kitchen.

Reporters greeted Nate and Misty as they left the apartment.

"We've been looking for Max," Nate said. "He wasn't answering his phone. We found him … dead already. That's all we know."

After stopping for hot chocolate at a drive-through coffee stand, Nate and Misty drove to police headquarters in silence.

Chief of Detectives, Fred Larsen, greeted them and then led them into his office and said, "Okay, let's begin at the beginning. Tell me all you know about Max White's death. Go back as far as you can."

Nate said, "How do you mean? Way back when I first met Max or just what happened tonight?"

"Well, you folks found his body, so you claim."

"What do you mean, so we claim? Of course we found his body. We called 911, didn't we?"

"Maybe I should explain. Both of you are not suspects. Today we simply say you're persons of interest."

An irritated Misty spoke up. "Persons of interest? That's insane. Max was Nate's manager. Have you heard of Nate Bradford? This is Nate. I just told you, Max was Nate's manager. Why are you being ridiculous?"

"Now, lady, calm down. What's your name?"

"Misty Wakefield's my name. Nate is my boyfriend. We loved Max. We went to check up on him."

Nate cut in. "You do know Max was one of the main owners of the arena that just burned down? He was depressed. Down in the dumps. Who wouldn't be when you lose your business?"

Misty said, "Maybe Max was drinking and fell. Can't you check that out?"

"Yeah, we'll do tests. You guys found him. Remember that."

Nate said, "Remember? How can we forget it? Max was the man who gave me my start in boxing.

He was like a father to me. He did tell me about some guys who were trying to bribe him into making someone throw a fight so they could win money. I guess it's okay to talk about it now. Max told me they were after me to lose a fight. But he never asked me to do anything illegal. Max would never have done that to me or with any guy he managed. He was a straight shooter. As a matter of fact, he just told me about it this morning. I had breakfast in his apartment. I was worried about Max. I know he was upset about the arena fire. Man, who wouldn't be?"

"Really," said Larsen. "Now, that's interesting. Yeah, that's mighty interesting. Why should I believe you?"

"Because I said so," Nate snapped. "Do we need a lawyer? Why are you doing this to us? I'm telling you, we opened his apartment door and found him lying on the floor. There was blood on a glass table. He fell."

Larsen said, "Or maybe was pushed."

"By whom? Who pushed him? Not us," Nate said in a more irritated tone.

"You just told me he might be having trouble with some hoods. Maybe they pushed him."

"Okay, so they pushed him. Why are you talking to us as if we did something to Max?" Nate said. "Anyway, the door was locked. We had to use a key. If any other guys were in there, they'd have left the door unlocked as they left. Right?"

• • •  187  • • •

"Look, I have to look into every angle. What else do you remember about those guys?"

"Max told me he never wanted me involved in any garbage. He even said he hoped I'd never hear about this, but he broke down and figured maybe I should know about this. I really didn't know what all that stuff was about. I was scared for both of us when I heard this."

"And?"

"And Max knew who the head of the gang was. He said he was going to have a talk with a man. I think his name is David Goldstein, a guy with the state boxing commission."

"I know Goldstein," Larsen said. "He's the Nevada State Boxing Commissioner. Did he see Goldstein?"

"I don't know. Max didn't want me upset. He said I had to have a clear mind. No tensions. He said he'd take care of things."

"Really. Well, I'll call Goldstein in the morning. If what you say is true, we'll have another suspect."

Misty cut in. "Another suspect? What's that supposed to mean? You said we weren't suspects."

"I mean we'll have another trail to follow. Maybe there's a link between Max White's death and those guys."

Nate argued, "Owens was the last guy I fought. Check with his manager and see if they approached Owens or him."

"I saw that fight you had," Larsen said. "I was there. It didn't look like either of you were going down, losing a fight on purpose. I thought it was a hell of a fight. Nobody would want to be beat up that way if they were going down for money."

Misty looked at Nate. "This is just another reason the boxing thing is evil. Didn't I tell you, Nate? It's a terrible thing to be involved with, make a career out of."

"I know, Misty, but Max told me he was handling things. He never asked me to do anything but get into fighting shape and be a big winner."

"Okay. You guys can handle that issue. I need to know exactly where you were all day today. You and Nate. Both of you."

Misty replied, "I was at work. I'm the head librarian at the main library here in town."

"Got proof?" Larsen asked.

"Of course I have proof. All you need to do is ask my workers. I was there all day," Misty said.

"We can check it out," Larsen said. He used his computer and typed in some words. "I just assigned Detective Tony Bianchi to check you out."

"This is ridiculous," Nate said. "My dad was a detective. He wouldn't have acted the way you're acting toward us."

"How do you know? If he was a good detective, he'd be doing just what I'm doing," Larsen said. "Go ask him."

"Nate can't. His dad was killed." Misty said.

"Well, I'm sorry about that. Really sorry."

"Then let us go home," Nate said. "It's been a tough couple days. We've done nothing but be concerned over Max. I just wish I'd have been with him all day. If he'd been drinking like your detective guys suspected, I could have prevented all of this. Do you have any idea how bad I feel, we feel?"

"Max was helping Nate get ahead in this world. I must admit, I hate, absolutely hate the business of boxing. But I love Nate. I supported his boxing, his fights, because I love him so much, and I cared for Max too."

"All right. All right. Then tell me what you saw when you entered Maxwell's apartment. How did you get in?"

"I had a key. I'm trying to tell you, Max was like a father to me. He was concerned about my life. I had a bum start in life after my dad died and my mother too," Nate told Larsen. "He trusted me. I trusted him. We were a team. He liked me more than all of his fighters. I just know this. He even bet on me when I fought."

Larsen said, "That's business, fella."

"It was more than business. It was like he adopted me."

"Adopted you? Since when does a fight promoter adopt a fighter?"

"You know what I mean," Nate fired back.

Misty cut in again. "Nate was hurt in his last fight with this man Owens. Did you know that? He landed in the hospital. Max was terrified. He told me this on the way to the hospital. We were right behind the ambulance. He told me how worried he was. So was I."

"I was there. I didn't know Nate was taken to the hospital until I heard it on the news. Did someone slip something into your water bottle?"

A really irritated Nate now stood up and said, "I got hit hard. You said you were there. What do you think we were doing, using feather dusters on each other? Listen, we went to check on Max. He gave me a key a while back. We opened the door, and Misty saw Max on the floor. She said, 'Oh, my God. Max is on the floor.' Now that's what happened. Check it out with your detectives that came in after we called 911. I'm telling you that's what happened. He must have fallen and hit his head on the glass table. How many times do we have to repeat this?"

"Calm down. Cool it. We'll check this out. Get out of here now and relax. If your story checks out, that's it. This is my job. Understand? Take this good-looking chick home. If you don't hear from my department again, that's it. Oh, yeah, I forgot to tell you. All of this was recorded. Okay with you?"

Nate said, "No. That's a sneaky trick. You're supposed to tell us that when we came in!"

"Look, I forgot. Okay? I forgot."

"That's bull."

Misty put her hands on Nate's chest. "It's okay, honey. He knows we didn't do anything. Let's go home."

A week later, Larsen called Nate. "You're clear, fella. Your story checked out. Max was filled with booze. The blood on the table was his, of course. We know he fell. There were no prints on his clothes other than his own. We know nobody pushed him unless they were wearing rubber gloves. We talked with Commissioner Goldstein and the arson guys. We're gonna make some arrests soon as we build a case against those morons."

"Thanks for the call. We're still upset over the way you treated us," Nate told Larsen.

There was no reply on the other end of the phone.

Nate told Misty. They readied for Max's memorial service. At the service, Larsen was there. Nate and Misty ignored him.

# CHAPTER THIRTY-TWO

**M**isty was talking quietly to Sue Ellen at their desks in the library. She had her cell phone in her purse, tucked under her desk. They both heard a muffled tone. Misty reached for her purse took out the phone and said, "This is Misty."

"Misty, I'm glad I'm able to reach you. This is Oscar. Misty, I'm afraid I have some news for you. It's not good.

"Oh, no, is it about my dad?"

"Yes. It looks like your dad may have suffered a stroke. An ambulance just took him to the hospital in Roseville."

"Oh my God! How bad is it?"

"Well, the medics assured me that for right now it's not too bad. He's conscious, but he's sort of in a daze. I'm not sure he recognized me. We were working in the hall when he suddenly sat down and looked kind of… out of it. He didn't answer me. I tried talking to him and, well, I got on the phone and called 911. The fire department guys got here first and a minute later an ambulance came."

"What hospital, Oscar? Which one?"

"It's Sutter Memorial, Misty. I'm jumping in the car now. I'll lock the hall up and get there right away. Don't worry. He's in good hands, and he'll be in good hands at the hospital."

"I'll catch a plane and be there as soon as possible. Give me a number where I can reach you. Can you pick me up at the airport?"

"You bet, Misty. Look, the medics said they have new medicines to use if it's a stroke. One told me he didn't appear too bad. Okay?"

"But I'm frightened. He's my father."

"Well, I'm gonna run now. You call me. Take care. Okay?"

Misty hung up.

"How bad is he?" Sue Ellen said.

"I don't know. The man told me he didn't think he was real bad. Oh, God, I hope not. Look, Sue Ellen, I'm calling Nate. I've got to be with my dad. I have to call an airline."

"Misty, if he's in a hospital there's nothing you

can do for him. Stay calm. I'm here. You get a flight and don't worry about this end of things."

Misty reached Nate and told him what had happened. Nate said he'd get two tickets for Sacramento right away and told Misty to pick him up.

Less than a half hour later, Misty parked outside Nate's apartment and ran in.

"How soon do we leave?"

"Three hours from now. I'm packed. Come on. Let's get to your place and get you ready."

While they were driving to the Vegas Airport, Misty's phone rang.

"Misty, it's Oscar. I'm at the hospital with your dad. He's gonna be okay. He's conscious. He knows where he is and has all of his bearings. They gave him a shot of something and, well, I guess it worked. But the doctor wants him to stay in the hospital for a couple days. Are you coming to see him?"

"Yes, Oscar. We're on the way to the airport. You're positive he's going to be okay?"

"Well, nobody can be positive about anything in this world, I guess, but from the looks of things, he'll be okay. I'd say this was just a real warning to slow down, take things easier."

"Oh, I'm so glad you called. I'll call you when we get to the airport. Our plane lands at six forty-eight."

"I'll be there. What airline?"

"Southwest. Thank you. See you there."

At a little past seven, Deering met Misty and Nate as planned. He reassured them that Byron appeared to be doing fine. But he confessed he had been scared stiff when Byron became ill.

"He's not even in cardiac care. I guess that's what they call that area. Your dad's in a regular private room. Have you folks eaten anything? Are you hungry?"

"We had some snacks," Nate said.

"Byron's resting. He knows you're coming. Let's get you some food."

Deering pulled into the parking area of a restaurant near the hospital, and the trio went inside for dinner. Deering talked about the goings on at the winery and how good business had been.

"Was Dad doing too much?" Misty said.

"You know your dad," Deering said. "He hands out assignments pretty good. But then he always involves himself in what's going on. Someone needs to tie him down. Sit on him. He's forever busy doing something."

Nate said, "Sometimes that's good. But, I guess you can overdo things. I ought to know."

"Byron talks about you, Nate, maybe more than you, Misty. I mean, he knows you're okay and have a good job, but he talks about Nate and his boxing. The one thing Byron is, well, he loves sports. He can talk all day about sporting events. He has me come over at night when things are quiet and we watch baseball, fights, even gets a kick out of the wrestling stuff."

Misty said, "I'm glad he gets his mind off work at least sometimes."

They left the restaurant and drove a few blocks to Sutter Hospital. Deering led them to the nurses' station and introduced Misty and Nate. Misty asked if it was all right to see her dad.

The nurse left for a minute and then came back. "He's dozing a bit, but he heard me come in his room. I asked him if he'd like to see you all. It's fine. Go ahead."

Misty gave Byron a kiss, and he smiled back at her.

"Oh, Dad, you scared us half to death. When Mr. Deering called, I was so frightened. What have you been up to?"

In a soft voice, Byron said, "I guess too much, accordin' to Oscar here and the doctors. But I'm fine. I feel a little bit like I got hit by a truck though. I'm okay. Really, I'm okay."

"Dad, I brought Nate along. He's here to help you and Mr. Deering."

Byron's gaze drifted to Nate. "I just kinda planned this here thing. Now I'm gonna sign you up to work for me. Sneaky way to do things, huh, Nate?"

"That works," Nate said. "Did you have a lot of tests today?"

JOEY CHISESI AND DIANE CHISESI

"Yep. They know my brain bettern' I do! Maybe that's why I'm kinda drained."

Misty spoke up. "Dad, remember the old joke? They X-rayed my brain today and they didn't find anything!"

"I used to tell that one all the time. Today it really happened," Byron said.

Deering added, "According to the docs, you're okay. They really didn't find anything, so far anyway, and they don't think they will."

"That's great news, Dad. Mr. Deering told us this on the ride from the airport."

"They said it was one of those TSAs that some people get. Byron's was one of those, maybe a little more than the usual. But he should be okay," Deering said.

"Maybe we should leave, Dad, I think you need to get some rest."

Deering said, "Forget your cares, Byron. Everything's in good hands."

Misty kissed her dad on his forehead. "Just relax, Dad. I'll be back tomorrow."

When they left Byron's room, Misty asked for a complete rundown on her dad's condition.

A nurse obliged her. "He's very fortunate. It was one of those small strokes, just enough to disable him for a few hours. The doctor believes he'll be fine. Doctor Thompson wants a few more tests done and to put him under observation here. We've got

● ● ●  198  ● ● ●

him on some medication, particularly a blood thinner. Like I say, Dr. Thompson believes he's going to be all right without impairment of any kind."

Deering said, "I'm glad. I told these folks the same thing."

Misty, a bit exhausted from the day's efforts, went to one of the guest bedrooms when they arrived at the house. She invited Nate to join her. She needed his comforting arms around her.

# CHAPTER THIRTY-THREE

Nate and Misty visited Byron each evening for the next three days. Byron appeared to be fine, even taking walks down the hospital corridors with them.

During the day, they worked with Deering at the winery. Everything appeared under control, including Byron's rapid recovery.

They insisted he remain quiet and relaxed in the hospital while they picked up his duties, most of which were overseeing other workers.

"You two make one great couple," Byron said one evening. I love to see you together. Yep, you're a doggone good team. You'd make great models for fashion magazines, well, not so much your clothes, but you're handsome, ya know, beautiful people."

He even hinted at their being married. Misty would respond each time with "I don't know if Nate could stand a nagging wife, particularly one who hates boxing."

On the fourth day after Byron's stroke, Misty received a call from the hospital.

Byron's primary nurse told Misty that Byron would be released from the hospital in the afternoon.

A delighted Misty said she and Nate would be there.

About two, Nate and Misty went to the nurses' station. She handed them two prescriptions for Byron. "Now make sure your dad takes these two medications just as it says on the instructions. He can go back doing anything he wishes. But the doctor's advice for him is to take it easy for another week or so. If he has any problems at all, make sure he calls his doctor right away. Okay? He's a fine gentleman and a lucky one to have both of you."

Misty thanked the nurse for helping her dad and promised that her dad would follow the doctor's orders.

"When he's ready to leave, just press his buzzer and we'll take him out to your car."

Misty and Nate walked down the hallway to Byron's room.

"Well, Dad, let's get you dressed and home. How are you feeling?

"Guys, I'm fine. I'm anxious to get home. I can see more channels on my TV. By the way, how's business?"

"Business is fine," Nate said. "Now don't start sweating about how business is. You need to come home and sit in the sunshine for a few days. We'll do the worrying."

Things went well. The winery doings continued on course, and Misty spoke to Nate about going back to Las Vegas. She talked with her dad and, to her delight, Byron said, "Do you think Nate could stay here for a few more days, Misty? Do you think he might be ready to work for me, I mean steady? Do you think I should ask him?"

"Dad, you're just full of questions, aren't you? Well, you know Nate's manager, Max, is gone. Oh, Dad, it was terrible. First the fire at the arena. Then Max died. Then you got sick."

"But I'm gonna be fine, just fine."

"You will be if you take things easier. You know, Dad, Nate may be ready for this. He just might. After dinner tonight I'll talk with him. He's pretty mellow with a full stomach."

"I'll leave things to you."

That evening, Misty told Nate about Byron's offer. "Nate, you really have no reason to come back to Las Vegas except to get your belongings together. You're through with your boxing career, aren't you?"

"The only reason to go back is you, Misty."

"I know, honey. I'll get your belongings together and send them back here for you. Remember, you put my name on your bank account? Well, I'll close out your account and send you the check. How does that sound? You have no contracts to honor. Right? You're really a very free man."

"You know, you're right. But I'll bet they have a boxing gym in Sacramento if I get the urge."

"Oh, no, Nate. Please don't think about that. Look, I'm thinking I can resign my job at the Vegas library and look for a job up here. Do you know how many libraries there are in this area? I'll bet I can land a good position with one of them, and not too far from here."

"I was afraid to bring it up, but we can be together, get married, that is, if you'll have me."

"Have you? Oh, Nate." She threw her arms around his neck. "I thought you'd never ask."

Misty called the airline agent the next day and managed to get a seat to Las Vegas.

At lunch with Byron and Nate, she told her dad about her plans.

Nate had a big grin on his face. "Byron, is that position you had open still available?"

Byron's smile was as big as Nate's. "I'll bet neither of you knew I planned getting sick on purpose so I'd get my daughter back home and with a big slug of a guy along with her."

"Dad, don't use the word slug around Nate. Those days are behind him. Right Nate?" Misty grinned at Nate.

• • •

Misty flew back to Las Vegas and made good on her promise to ship Nate's things to him in Newcastle. She closed out his bank account and sent him the funds. She managed to break the lease on Nate's apartment after paying a month's rent as a penalty.

They talked to each other each day by cell phone. Nate kept telling her they were acting like high school kids.

Misty kept getting good reports from Nate on her dad's health. She felt good hearing that. Nate assured her that all was going well business wise at the Wakefield Vineyard and Winery.

In two months' time, Misty landed work at a library in Roseville. Leaving her fellow workers at the Las Vegas Main Library wasn't easy. But she managed to do it. The Vegas library threw a party for her right after work hours just before she finished packing for the moving company. Bravely, she drove her car from Vegas to Newcastle, stopping one night in Carson City, Nevada.

When she arrived at her dad's home, Nate and her dad gave her a great welcome. She knew for sure that she'd made the right decision.

# CHAPTER THIRTY-FOUR

B yron's close call and the tragic death of Max found Nate wondering often if the Seattle Police Department, in particular the detective bureau, had made progress solving his parents' deaths.

It had now been twelve years since his parents disappeared. Only on rare occasions had Nate called back to Seattle to ask his Uncle Ted about the case. When he phoned Uncle Ted, he received updates on the never-ending investigation of the tragedy. *Maybe,* thought Nate, *the Seattle Police Force saw fit to keep the manslaughter file alive.* He clung to that hope.

Nate felt that victims were just that, victims,

never to live, forever gone. But solving a crime offered some resolution, some solace. Time helped too as a healer.

It was Misty who often spoke to Nate about the death of his parents and the separation from his sister.

At times, when Nate spoke of his childhood and the awful news of his parents' failure to return home from their Sunday afternoon boat ride on Shilshole Bay, Misty would console Nate with her philosophical belief that there was no time limit on grief.

Misty had provided Nate with strength that steered him toward becoming a clear-headed thinker. Misty's support had helped Nate even after the nightmarish life he'd led.

The two of them were driving in Byron's car to Lincoln for some shopping when Nate, hand on the steering wheel, said, "You know, Misty, I haven't heard from Detective Jennings for a couple months. I can't imagine anything's new, but remind me to give him a call when we get back home."

Misty reached for the radio control to turn the volume down. At that moment, they heard the familiar sound of the cell phone playing the theme song from *Rocky*. Misty said, "Remind me to get rid of that music. I'll replace it with the 'William Tell Overture' or something like that."

In disbelief, Misty answered the phone and said,

"Detective Jennings, you will never, I mean never, ever believe what just happened.

Nate just asked me to remind him to call you when we get back home."

Misty laughed at something the detective said.

A stunned Misty shouted, "Oh my God. Wait, Detective Jennings, I'm going to give you over to Nate."

With that, she said, "Nate, pull over. Quick. Pull over."

"Let me find a safe place so I can get off the road. Tell Jennings to hold on."

Nate maneuvered the car to a wide siding, hit the brakes, and stopped. Flipping the switch to the emergency flashers, he reached for the cell phone. "Hello, Uncle Ted. This is Nate. What's happening?"

"I've got what appears to be a major break in the case, Nate. It's still unfolding as I talk to you, but this looks very promising. Look, I know you're on the road somewhere. I'd like to tell you the story. Can you get back to me in a couple of hours? The story's a bit long. I'm fending off the news vultures now. How they get these leaks I'll never know. Okay with you? Nate, are you there? Nate?"

Stunned, Nate finally managed a response. "Yeah, Uncle Ted. I'm here. I heard you. I don't know what to say right now."

"Well," Jennings said, "just relax and do what you were going to do."

"Yes, okay."

"Talk to you later."

Nate handed the cell phone to Misty. "My God, Misty, can you believe this?"

"Yes, I can, honey. You know how hard Jennings worked on the case all these years. Let's get to the store and back to the winery."

"Is this real or what? Are we dreaming?"

"Are you okay to drive? You're not in shock, are you?" Misty said.

"No, no, I'm fine. I have to admit I'm stunned. I guess I never thought I'd be hearing those words."

"Well, tonight we'll hear the whole story."

At six, Nate dialed Detective Jennings. A police clerk responded and, hearing Nate's request, put the call through to Jennings's extension.

As though he'd been waiting by the phone, Jennings said, "Hello, Nate. Right on time. Well, I have more to my story for you. We've got a confession."

Nate felt overcome with emotion.

"You know, Nate, I almost feel sorry for this guy. The accident's been eating away at his insides all these years."

"What's his name?"

"Oh, yeah. His name's Tim Ford. He lives in a Seattle suburb. He's married. Got two kids. His wife, Melissa, claims it's the absolute truth. She's quite a nice woman, by the way. It seems he and three friends were joy riding and drinking beer.

First of all, that's a felony, drinking and driving and piloting a watercraft. The law's the same as on land."

"Okay," Nate said. He could hear Misty sigh on the extension phone.

Ted continued. "Anyway, it appears this guy dropped his passengers off at a dock and then, like a crazy fool, he took off for a spin by himself, circling around a couple miles or so in the Sound. Being drunk out of his skull, he opened the throttle. Visibility was getting worse by the minute. He rammed into your dad's boat. The impact was so great, it literally ripped your dad's boat in half, but drunk or not drunk, this Ford guy never lost control of his craft. He thinks he went over the *Johnny O* and continued to speed away. He said he'd heard TV news reports about a terrible accident at sea. The reports mentioned the name of the sunken craft. It was the *Johnny O.* He figured that was the craft he rammed."

At this point, Nate cut in. "My, God, didn't he know enough to go back and see what he did?"

"He claims he was too plastered and at the same time scared silly. He couldn't react. He just kept going. How he found the dock where he dropped the other three off, he doesn't know. It was almost completely dark by then, and he and the other guy and two gals with them had trouble getting the boat out of the water and onto the boat trailer."

"Anyway, he claims he drove the other three people to one of the gal's homes, dropped them off, and headed to his house where he kept the boat garaged."

Jennings story continued. He told Nate that the guy sobered up enough the next day to be able to go to school, a junior college. He'd never checked on any possible damage to his boat for days, just blocked everything out.

"Know what I mean?" Jennings said.

"Been there and done that," Nate replied.

Then Jennings told Nate how, at the time of the accident, he and other detectives canvassed all the businesses in the area looking for evidence of people buying boat waxes, scratch kits, damage kits, repair kits, any kind of boat repair materials. All their leads turned into nothing. Months later, this guy traveled to Spokane to get repair materials. Since he kept the boat stored in his parents' garage with a cover over the damaged bow, there was no reason for his folks to know what he'd done. It was fall, and the guy never took the craft out for months.

"So that's why you couldn't find anyone buying repair stuff around the Seattle area," Nate said.

"Right. We put out feelers to all stores in Washington, but it doesn't mean everyone looked at them."

"Uh-huh, okay," Nate put in. "Then what?"

"Well, according to Ford, he'd go out to the

garage, turn on a portable heater, and work on repairing the bow. The craft was fiberglass, so he claims he searched the Internet to learn how to repair a fiberglass boat."

Jennings paused. "But now comes the real interesting thing, the main reason this chap turned himself in. Seems what he'd done bugged him all these years and affected what he did from time to time."

Jennings continued. "He told us that on his honeymoon on a tour bus with his new bride, Melissa, he began making comments about his past drinking days."

"Really," cut in Misty, still on the extension phone. "That's beginning to sound terribly sad."

"Yes, it's sad all right. Their honeymoon started here in Seattle with a flight to Los Angeles. There they boarded a tour bus for Disneyland and ultimately Las Vegas."

"Las Vegas," exclaimed Nate. "Was this Melissa he married one of the passengers on the craft that ran down my folks?"

"No, but he dropped his boat companions off his buddy list and went out of his way to ignore them in the months that followed. Well, this Ford guy was trying to make the honeymoon something special for his bride; at least he thought he was. Melissa tells me he actually threw some money out of a tour bus they were on as a joke. He thought he was being funny and wanted to give everybody a laugh."

"What!" Nate shouted over the phone. "Like a dollar bill? No, it couldn't be, just couldn't be!"

"I don't know, Nate. Why? What's a dollar bill got to do with this?"

"See if you can find out, Mr. Jennings. I'm probably crazy, but, well, I'll tell you later."

"Okay. I'll see if she knows. Anyway, she wondered why her husband talked about his past in such a negative way from time to time." Jennings went on. "The people that night were, so to speak, innocent, although they should never have been drinking.

"Ford's wife tried to prod him into talking about whatever was bothering him. But she wasn't getting very far with her probing. She told us, of her own volition, that he'd murmur in his sleep and wake up with cold sweats. She'd try her best to console the guy, but things were slipping between them as far as caring and feelings were concerned. He was in sales for his company, and his sales were going downhill. He began to hit the bottle again. They're both Catholic, so she suggested he see a priest."

"Wow," Misty said. "That must have been an awful way to live."

Jennings explained that the guy did see a priest. But he twisted the story he told the priest just enough to avoid the truth, like he'd damaged a boat. "He may or may not have been aware that the priest couldn't tell us Ford confessed to a really serious crime."

"If he had a good Catholic upbringing, he'd have known about church confidentiality," Misty said.

"Honestly, the guy's not your regular tough guy. He made a mistake, a bad mistake. Now, he's going to have to face the consequences. Actually, the guy's a rat for handling a horrible situation like he did. He had no feelings about what he did when he did it. He left you and your sister hanging all these years. He'll pay for this. I'll make him pay," Jennings said.

"But, anyway, Ford's sales were going down the toilet. His sales manager called Melissa and told her he was worried. Melissa asked what her husband could do. Ford's job record had been good, so his boss said they should get him some help. Between them, they thought psychiatric treatment might be the answer if Ford agreed."

"Did he go?" Misty said.

"Yeah, he saw the doc a half dozen times. The doctor put him on antidepressants. I guess Ford never fessed up to him either. Well, Ford's wife said that about two o'clock one morning, he broke down. She was scared stiff. He cried like a baby and blurted out the whole horrible story to her. He said he was a young, stupid guy out having fun. He didn't mean to harm anyone."

"Oh, I can believe that," Nate said, "You know

this situation might never have been resolved. This could have gone on forever. Am I right?"

"You're a hundred percent accurate, right on the money," Jennings said. "Sometimes breaks in a case come from the strangest places and in the strangest ways."

"What'll happen to this man?" Misty said.

"He'll be charged with two counts of man-slaughter. It's serious. Even though he confessed, he'll have to stand trial. There's no need for a jury. This can be heard by a judge."

"Will we have to come to Seattle?" Nate's voice shook as he thought of having to sit in a courtroom and look at the Ford guy.

"Only if you want to see justice done. I don't know your mind-set after all these years. You can pitch the judge to throw the book at this guy or you can appeal to the judge for leniency. I think the guy needs to pay big. The ball's in your court now."

Misty said, "Is he locked up?"

"Yes, I'm afraid so," Jennings replied. "A judge set bail at two hundred thousand. To post a bond would cost him and his family twenty grand. He settled for a court appointed attorney, a woman. Sharp too."

"What does this all mean?"

"First off, his trial could be swift. As I say, it all depends on what the judge decides about his pun-ishment. Ford's attorney will tell the judge how this guy has suffered already. The district attorney will say he hasn't suffered enough."

"Wow," Misty said. "What a tough situation all the way around."

Almost at the same time, Nate said, "I longed for a solution. I wanted whoever did this to pay and pay. Who'd ever guess he turns out to be a guy with two young kids and a good wife?"

"Know how you feel, folks. But now you have to talk it over. Get back to me as soon as you can."

"Okay, Uncle Ted. Will do," Nate said. "Thanks for everything."

"Yes, thanks Mr. Jennings," Misty added.

As Jennings began to hang up, Nate said, "Oh, Uncle Ted, you made a comment about this fellow's tossing money out a bus?"

"Yeah. His wife mentioned it."

"Look, this sounds crazy, but ask her to pin down the date, will you?" Nate said.

"Will do."

"Thanks for all your work."

They ended their phone conversation.

A perplexed look covered Nate's face.

"Nate, it will be all right. Everything will work out okay. We'll go to this man's trial."

Nate sat transfixed. He hadn't said a word. Finally he spoke. "I can't really believe this is happening."

"Honey, it's been sixteen years. It's almost as if

someone has been seriously ill for a long time and then one day passes away. When the death occurs, it's still a shock. So your feelings are normal, totally understandable."

Nate became silent again. Then he looked into her eyes and said, "How can I show mercy for this man? How can I be sympathetic? Yet, how can I be cruel toward him? He's married. He's the father of two kids. If he goes to prison, those kids won't have a father. That'll make things just as bad as life was for Terri Jo and me."

"Let's just wait to hear from Detective Jennings," Misty suggested. "You don't have to make a decision this very moment. How about we tell Dad about everything? It's surprising what another day brings in the thought process, especially when you discuss things with someone who understands. Anyway, let's go for a walk while it's still light outside. Or better yet, let me put a little supper together for all of us. How about it, Nate? Okay?"

During supper, Misty, her dad, and Nate discussed the sudden turn of events. Nate listened for any indication of Byron's sentiments regarding the pending trial of Tim Ford.

Byron appeared to be leaning toward leniency. He tied his beliefs to religious philosophies. At one point during dinner, Byron cited the biblical principle that vengeance belonged to God and to God alone. "Vengeance is mine and mine alone, God said," Byron quoted.

At that point, Nate asked Byron, "Do you suppose God knows the suffering my sister and I endured?"

"Yes, I'm sure God knows. Remember, God would never put a heavy load upon you that you couldn't carry," Byron replied. "Look at it this way. You're here in our home in these beautiful surroundings with two beautiful people." Byron grinned.

Nate produced a faint smile. "You know, you're right. I have Misty now. And I have you, Byron, a genuine surrogate father."

Misty rose from her chair, bent over, and kissed Nate.

Byron said, "I'm blessed also. I have the two of you."

Misty said, "See, God works in mysterious ways."

"If only my sister could share this with me, I'd feel better, maybe even have sympathy for this Ford fellow," Nate said.

"Someday, Nate, you'll find her. I feel it with all my heart and soul," Misty said.

"If you feel it in your bones too, it's probably arthritis," Byron said.

# CHAPTER THIRTY-FIVE

Another week went by. Byron continued to improve. Nate learned more and more about the business of grape growing and winery operations.

Nate and Misty continued to discuss the coming trial. Nate felt torn between mercy and sternness. Byron held steadfast to his beliefs concerning compassion. Misty leaned toward compassion but wouldn't force her feelings on Nate.

The phone rang one night. Misty took the call. She beckoned to Nate to come to the phone, whispering Jennings's name to him. Jennings told Nate a preliminary hearing date had been set for Ford, but

Nate didn't have to be there. Jennings figured Ford's trial date would be set to begin in a month or so.

"You can come up at that time, Nate," Jennings said. "Oh, by the way, have you considered what stance you're going to take if we call you up for a statement on sentencing? Even though you didn't witness the accident, it's possible the district attorney may call you anyway if need be. But mainly you'll be called upon at sentencing time. I believe the judge may be a woman. Sometimes I've found female judges to be a bit more lenient. I hear she's very fair, but a stickler with the law. I can't help but feel your position on sentencing will contribute to her mind-set."

When the conversation was over, Nate filled Misty in with the information Jennings had for him.

"We still need to wait till the actual trial date is set. I just hope there'll be no delays or postponements."

And for one of the very rare moments surrounding the whole terrible episode, Nate grinned as he said, "Will God's call come in on our cell phone or on the Wakefield Winery line?"

Misty laughed. "See, you're already getting a message."

"Sure wish we had a better connection."

Misty threw her arms around him. "Oh, Nate, I do love you so."

Nate took her face between his hands and kissed her forehead, then her nose, and finally her lips.

# CHAPTER THIRTY-SIX

nother ten days went by without a call from Jennings. On the eleventh day, he called from Seattle. But all three—Nate, Misty, and Byron—were in town away from the house phone. When they returned, they found a message. Nate called the number Jennings left, but Jennings didn't answer.

The next morning, Nate tried again, and this time reached a desk sergeant who promised to get a message through to Jennings. It was about a half hour later when Jennings returned the call.

"Got a few minutes?" he said to Nate.

"Sure have, Uncle Ted."

Jennings said that the trial date had been set.

Ford had pled guilty at the preliminary because of being drunk. Now they have to have the formality of a trial. The judge will ask Ford once more how he pleads and if it's the same as the preliminary, the judge will accept it. Then she'll ask for statements from injured parties. That will be you regarding sentencing. Follow all of this, Nate?"

Nate assured Jennings he understood.

Jennings went on. "Okay. So the trial date is set for one month from now."

Nate interjected, "One month? Why so long?"

"Well, the judge has to give the attorney time to prepare a defense in case Ford changes his mind. See, she'll look up similar cases and see what sentences were imposed. Don't forget, she's got other cases she's working on. Usually the judge'll talk with the attorneys and set a tentative date, one that all parties can live with. Anyway, the date is August seventh. Better write that down. This gives you time to get airline tickets, or you can take a nice train ride. I understand AMTRAK runs from your neck of the woods right to Seattle. Either way, you got time to get tickets. I assume Misty and you will come up here. Right?"

"Oh, sure, Uncle Ted. We'll be there; although, it's right close to harvest time for the grapes. I guess you probably know we're handling Misty's dad's vineyard and winery for him. He's made a great recovery from a little stroke he had, but we're trying to make his life easier for him."

"Yep, I know where you are. Remember, I'm a detective." Jennings continued. "I'll send you a letter with all the details. The case has drawn some attention, come to think of it. There could be a number of people in the courtroom. I'll get some official papers that'll guarantee you and Misty seats right behind the prosecuting attorney's desk. I'll be so happy to see you, Nate. And I can't wait to meet Misty. She sounds beautiful. I'll bet she is."

"Oh, yes. She's gorgeous. Every one who meets her thinks she's beautiful. I'm so lucky. Oh, oh, she heard what I said. Guess what? She's blushing." She'll just get conceited if I brag about her any more. Uncle Ted, thank you. We'll be there on the seventh of August."

Nate hung up. "I've a lot to tell you, Misty, but first we need to get two airline tickets to Seattle right away. Or he said we could relax a little and take a train ride up and back. Let's ask your dad where the AMTRAK station is. That could make our decision a little easier. What would you like to do? Fly or take a train ride?"

"A train ride sounds interesting. I'll bet the scenery is gorgeous, but that'll take us away from here for a couple more days. Maybe we better fly."

"Okay. Let's get working on the tickets and hope there'll be no delays in that fellow's trial."

The day before the trial, Nate and Misty arrived at the Sacramento Airport, proceeded through the inspection process, and found two seats alongside each other in the departure area of Alaska Airlines. Misty was attempting to relax Nate by making small talk.

"Funny thing, Nate. We're traveling on Alaska Airlines, and it's hotter than all get out in Sacramento." She reached for Nate's hand. "Honey, have you decided what you're going to say to the judge?"

Nate halfway nodded, but he didn't give Misty a direct answer. "Whatever you say to him is okay."

Finally, an announcement came. "Now boarding for Seattle, flight number three ninety-four." They waited until their row was called and boarded the jet.

The flight took about one and a half hours, landing at SETAC Airport, the symbol for Seattle and Tacoma, Washington. They picked up their luggage, found their car rental agent, left the airport, and headed for their hotel.

"It's been a while since I've been here," Nate said. "I wonder if there are any big changes in Seattle. The weather sure is decent. It must be fifteen degrees cooler than Sacramento. I guess I miss that."

"This is my first time ever in Seattle. It's a lovely city. Too bad we're here for such an unpleasant reason," Misty said.

Their hotel room had a small balcony with a view of Seattle's famous Space Needle. The two stood together holding hands as Nate pointed out other landmarks.

"Seems like a long dream, sometimes a nightmare, since I left here." Nate looked into Misty's expressive eyes.

"Oh, so I'm part of your nightmare, am I?"

"No, no, Mist. You're the dream part, the nicest dream a fellow could have."

"You know, Nate, I love it when you call me Mist."

"Well, guess what? We're in misty Seattle, so Mist just seemed appropriate."

"I think you swallowed a dictionary. You sound so cultured."

"I am." Nate said, "You're finally noticing it? It's about time."

# CHAPTER THIRTY-SEVEN

The next morning, Nate and Misty found Seattle's Municipal Court Building, cleared security, and looked at the schedule of hearings and trials set for August seventh. Tim Ford's trial was to begin at ten thirty in courtroom number three.

Detective Ted Jennings stood outside the courtroom door. Nate recognized him as Jennings broke into a big smile and grabbed Nate's hand. Jennings spoke first. "Nate, you look great. I bet this beautiful lady with you deserves the credit. Right?"

"Uncle Ted, this is Misty, my right arm, my left arm, everything. Isn't she something?"

"You're everything Nate said you were and more."

Misty blushed.

"Can you imagine a pretty woman like she is blushing so easy?"

Jennings smiled. He paused a moment and then said, "Let's get inside. The judge is just finishing up the case before Ford's. I'll show you where to sit until the bailiff calls Ford's case. I'll sit with you, and then we'll move to different seats when she finishes up with the case she's hearing now."

Ted smiled at Nate. "Oh, look. This case is just about finished. Ford should be coming in any minute now. There's his wife over there. She's very nice, an absolutely decent lady."

Jennings nodded toward a redheaded woman seated with two men and two women. One of the women was holding Melissa Ford's hand.

The sight of Melissa Ford and the anguish showing on her face struck Nate as Misty said, "Oh, God, I feel so bad for her. How terribly sad."

Almost at the same moment, a bailiff appeared from a rear door holding Tim Ford's arm.

"That's him, folks. That's Ford," Ted said, emotion showing in his voice. "He did a bad thing, and now he's paying the price. The question for the judge will be how to punish Ford for his deeds, plus his failure to face the music. You probably won't find any legal precedence for delaying a confession because a crime is a crime."

Nate had been silent. How could he ask the judge to be lenient when Ford took his life away from him for so many years? Ford's actions dealt Nate a horrible blow—took his childhood, his sister, and his mom and dad's love. Nate felt rage fill his body.

"There'll probably be a couple minutes' delay, what with Ford's attorney and the prosecuting attorney visiting up there with the judge. Wouldn't surprise me at all if they go into the judge's chamber for a conference. Yep, sure enough, there they go. Let's hope they knock that off in a hurry."

Misty said, "Yes, let's hope."

Nate heard Jennings's words, but they didn't mean much to him. He needed to get control of his anger so he could find the right things to say to the judge.

Nate said, "I guess I've spent a part of my life trying to avoid courtrooms. I don't like any part of this one either."

Misty took Nate's hand. "Try and relax, honey. I know this is awfully hard for you."

"I wish my folks were still alive," Nate said.

A bailiff announced case number three forty-six, the City of Seattle and County of King versus Timothy James Ford.

"Well, that was luck. That was quick," Jennings said.

The judge, a woman in her early fifties with blond hair, touched the gavel to her desk, and spoke. "I'm Judge Jane Albright of the Municipal Court of the City of Seattle. It is my understanding that the plaintiff, Mr. Ford, wishes to enter a plea in this case. Am I correct, Mr. Ford?

Ford nodded his head.

"I need your verbal response, Mr. Ford. Please speak up so the courtroom may hear your voice."

"Yes, Your Honor."

Judge Albright looked at Ford's defense attorney, Donna Green. "Are you prepared to enter a plea on behalf of your client, Miss Green?"

Donna Green stood up. "Your Honor, Timothy Ford wishes to plead guilty to first-degree manslaughter."

Judge Albright looked at Ford and attorney Green, hesitated for a moment, and then said, "It appears to the court that you're complying with your preliminary plea. Am I correct, Miss Green?"

"Yes, Your Honor."

After a pause, Judge Albright said, "Before I impose the sentence upon the defendant, Timothy Ford, I will hear statements from all concerned in this matter. First, Ms. Green, do you have persons to come forth on behalf of Mr. Ford concerning this sentencing?"

"I do," answered Green. Ford's defense attorney walked to the judge's bench and handed Judge Albright a paper that contained the names of those who would speak.

Because appeals for leniency required no oaths, Green called her first person, Jack Wenthrop, Tim Ford's sales manager. Wenthrop chose to stand before Judge Albright.

"I'm here to tell the court about Tim Ford's excellent character. He has been with our company, Future Information, for twelve years. He's represented our Seattle-based firm as a salesman for the past ten years, and Tim holds a spotless record of honesty and integrity. Tim possesses an excellent knowledge of our products and goes out of his way to assist our customers whenever they require additional attention."

Wenthrop said that Tim's sales had slackened over the past year. He said he felt Tim appeared under duress at times and had tried to ply the reasons for the stress from him. "But he always attempted to deflect the questions. He told me he'd be fine soon. I asked him about his marriage. He said his marriage was perfect. He did admit he was having trouble sleeping."

Wenthrop ended his appeal by saying, "Future Information will try to hold a space for Tim no matter what the outcome of the trial."

Defense Attorney Green then called upon a

secretary who had worked with Ford for the past eight years. She corroborated much of what Wentworth had stated. "He was always a gentleman and very intelligent. I enjoyed working with him."

Prosecuting Attorney Rogers seemed surprised when Green asked Larry Atherton to come forward. Greene informed Judge Albright that Atherton had been a passenger in the boat just before Ford took off for his final daredevil dash in the craft that struck the *Johnny O* and caused the deaths of Johnny and Priscilla Bradford.

Atherton, smartly dressed in a pin-striped black business suit, told Judge Albright that Ford and the other boat passengers had been drinking heavily prior to Ford's wild ride. However, he noted that Ford, then a close friend, was not used to such a drinking binge. In fact, Atherton, now an ophthalmologist, claimed none of the foursome, including himself, were known as heavy drinkers.

"I don't have the faintest idea why we did what we did that day. I only wish I could have prevented that final water madness from taking place. Tim Ford was simply not the kind of guy who would intentionally hurt anybody. I know we lost touch with each other after that, but I can't see how Ford could possibly have changed much over the years."

And then Green asked Melissa's sister, Pamela Emerson, to come forward and speak. Emerson told of Ford's relationship with her and the rest of Melissa's family, pointing out only good things about Ford, including his being a wonderful husband to Melissa and a great father to their children.

Finally, Greene called out the name of Melissa Ford. She walked to the table where her husband was seated.

Judge Albright repeated Melissa's name and invited her to come forward. She observed a very nervous woman walking to the witness chair.

Visibly shaking, Melissa sat down.

With tears streaming down her face, Melissa began to speak. She related what she had told the police about the stress her husband had experienced a few years following their marriage. She broke down a few times, and Judge Albright gave her time to compose herself. But as the words streamed from her, she lowered her voice to an almost whisper. Judge Albright patiently urged her several times to speak up as best she could.

Melissa told of the steady decline in her husband's confidence level until his final breakdown and confession. Her final words were a ringing, "I love Tim. What will happen to me and my children?"

Observers in the courtroom were moved to tears.

Nate found it impossible to read anything in Judge Albright's face. During Melissa Ford's appeal for clemency, he noticed how the judge looked down at the witness chair and other times how the judge seemed to gaze outward as if contemplating facts in the case.

When Melissa Ford finished her appeal, Defense Attorney Green thanked her as she rose from the witness chair and walked back to her place behind her husband.

Judge Albright then declared a fifteen-minute recess.

Nate, Misty, and Jennings remained seated at the prosecuting attorney's table. Nate noticed moisture around Misty's eyes, not uncommon for Misty. She dabbed them with a handkerchief and turned her head somewhat away from Nate's gaze, as if to say, "Nate, I don't want to influence you in any way when you speak to the judge today."

After fifteen minutes, Judge Albright reentered the courtroom and took her position at the bench. She declared, "We will now hear from prosecuting attorney, Kenneth Rogers. Mr. Rogers, I have your list. Will you call your first speaker, sir?

Kenneth Rogers stood to announce the name of Detective Ted Jennings. Jennings hurried to the front of the courtroom. He asked the judge if he could sit in the witness chair. She obliged him.

Jennings began his comments by telling of the years he worked with Johnny Bradford. He told brief yarns of their exploits as a detective team on the Seattle Police Force. He said, "I was heartbroken by the splitting up of the Bradford children and their having to be placed in the custody of foster parents. I wanted so much to bring to justice the killer or killers of the Bradfords."

He lowered his voice. "When I learned of Tim Ford's confession, I was overjoyed, hoping justice would be served. I still hold to that emotion and understand that justice will be served when the penalty is imposed by you, Judge Albright. But I must admit now that my desires have been tempered somewhat, maybe by the passage of time. Again, I know you have your duty to impose as stern a penalty as the law provides. And it's my duty to ask you to hold Mr. Ford to a severe sentencing. I hope I'm not confusing the court with my statements."

With that, Jennings rose from the witness chair and moved back to the prosecuting attorney's table. He put his head down to his chest and seemed to want to avoid all possible eye contact.

Prosecutor Rogers then called on detectives Carron and Forrestor. Each reiterated Jennings's thoughts. They told of their feelings about Tim Ford. They spoke of their overwhelming anger over the deaths of the Bradfords, particularly their fellow police detective, Johnny Bradford.

During Carron's comments, he looked at Judge Albright and asked, "How are we supposed to show sympathy for Ford's actions? Didn't he have years to step forward and admit his guilt? We lived with his actions too. Ford didn't show sympathy to us.

How many killers show remorse? They only think of themselves. I'm sorry all this ever took place. But we live with the consequences of other people's horrible actions."

He left his testimony there and returned to his seat in the courtroom. Forrestor essentially made the same statement only in his own words.

Rogers arose again and said, "I now call Nate Bradford."

As Nate rose, a sudden cry came from the back of the courtroom. A beautiful, dark-haired young woman who had been seated alone in the rear of the courtroom came rushing forward toward Nate. She threw her arms about his neck and continued to call his name aloud. "Nate, Nate, oh, Nate. Is it you? Is it really you? Oh, God! Nate, Nate." She was sobbing at the same time.

Two bailiffs rushed to where Nate and the woman were standing, ready to pull the young woman away from Nate. At that point, Judge Albright pounded her gavel on her desk and called, "Order! Order! Order in the court."

At the same time, the woman cried out, "It's me. Nate, it's me, Terri Jo. Your sister."

The occupants of the courtroom, totally overcome with emotion, became completely quiet. The only sounds heard were those of Nate and Terri Jo as she continued to weep.

"Terri Jo. Oh, God, it is you. I can't believe my eyes. Terri Jo, my little sister."

Judge Albright called out, "This court is adjourned for two hours. We'll take a lunch break." She hit the gavel on the desk, stood up, and as she did, dabbed her eyes with a small kerchief in the sleeve of her judicial robe.

Nate held Terri Jo, tears welling in his eyes.

Ted and Misty stood close by.

It was Jennings who finally broke the silence by saying, "This is wonderful, folks. Let's celebrate. Come on, let's have a great lunch."

The foursome left the courtroom.

Across the street from the courthouse, they found a cozy restaurant, ironically called The Justice.

"This seems appropriate," said Jennings as he asked the hostess for a table.

Everyone wanted to hear all about Terri Jo's life—where had she lived, who were her foster parents, what was she doing now?

The questions came in a rush too fast for her to answer. At last, Terri Jo began her story. She hated being a foster child even though she had no problems with her foster parents. What she wanted more than anything was to study commercial art.

Terri Jo had always had a flair for art. She could draw a portrait of anyone in minutes. Her art teachers had always encouraged her talent, suggesting she go to fairs and do portraits of folks.

On more than one occasion, Terri Jo drew caricatures of her foster parents and hid them. But every now and then, she'd have a new set of parents who would punish her for poking fun at them.

As a result of the assistance she received from her school counselors, she was offered a scholarship in a work study program at the University of Northern Colorado in Greeley.

At the same time, Terri Jo was accepted at the distinguished Bemis School of Art in Colorado Springs. School officials at UNC suggested she take the Bemis summer program. Her UNC art scholarship included room and board in Colorado Springs. She had selected boarding in a home near the art school.

"I buried myself in my studies, but as a consequence, I lost contact with everyone in Seattle, including Nate."

Terri Jo's emotions began to show, Nate noticed. She seemed both excited and remorseful.

Nate could hardly hold back his feelings. "I'm so proud of you, Terri Jo," he said over and over. "Oh, my God, I had no idea you were in Colorado. I tried to find you using the Internet, but it was as though you'd disappeared off the face of the earth."

"Speaking of the Internet," Terri Jo said, "That's how I found out about this trial. I was reading a local newspaper on the net and came across the story about a man's confession to a crime twelve years ago. There was our name, Bradford, even a reference to you and me, Nate. When I learned the date of the trial, I decided to take the train ride to Seattle."

I tried to relax and enjoy the scenery, but I was so nervous. I missed a lot of the gorgeous views. I thought how beautiful it would be to capture some of those sights on canvas."

Before anyone knew it, two hours had passed.

Jennings insisted on paying the bill. "My treat," he said. The four of them headed back to the courthouse.

On the way, Jennings asked Nate if he had come to a decision about what he would say to the judge.

"You know, I've run this through my mind over and over, but I still don't know."

Back in the courtroom, Judge Albright took her place and said, "I'd like to tell the Bradfords how happy I am for their reunion. If any good comes from this hearing, it's that. Congratulations to you both." Then Judge Albright invited Nate to give his statement.

Nate chose to stand before the judge. "I've dealt with this situation for some time," Nate said. "In my mind, I pictured the day I'd find out who took away my parents lives. I imagined what I would do. You know, Your Honor, I may have left a short boxing career behind me, and I believe I'm looking toward a new life. But, before that, my life was in shambles. Then good men and a great lady turned my life around. I guess what I'm trying to say is if I had the killer in front of me, I'd pound him to death with my bare fists."

Nate paused and then continued. "In my mind, I saw the killer put behind bars forever. I saw him being executed. I can't help saying that. Many times my mind flashed back to the day my folks disappeared. I relived that day over and over again. And now, the day has finally come. Mr. Ford is here for all of us to see, maybe to hate, maybe to pity. As I stand here I must admit, just minutes ago I told this to Detective Jennings. I now have terribly mixed emotions. That may be hard for you to believe, Your Honor, but I do. I really do."

Turning around, Nate went on. "See, there he is in handcuffs. Look at his face. Look at his wife's face. Well, it may be getting to me. It's like I'm doing a hundred and eighty turn around, if you know what I mean. I see myself twelve years ago when this went down and what it meant to me. But now I can put myself in Ford's place and the horrific spot his wife and kids will be in."

Nate paused for a moment. "Then I turn it around and say to myself, this guy let me hang for twelve years. He let me suffer. Look what I lived through. Well, Judge, you don't know my entire background. Only a few people really know. But I survived. I made it through. Today, I found my sister. At lunch, I found out she suffered the same way I did, although it looks like she handled it better than me. She doesn't know all this yet."

Nate paused once again. He shuffled his feet, trying to get a hold of his emotions. "I have seen the turmoil Mr. Ford's wife is going through, and I can see the struggles the Ford children will face with their dad in prison. And you know Tim Ford has had to suffer too for what he did, holding it inside himself for all these years. Everyone has had to deal with the consequences of his actions and . . . am I rambling?"

"It's all right. Please continue, Mr. Bradford," Judge Albright said.

"But seeing his wife, hearing of all the anguish they've been through because he drank too much one Sunday afternoon and caused a terrible accident, I'm now convinced he's suffered enough. In his own way, he slipped to the depths of despair and brought his wife and children down with him. Everyone involved has suffered enough."

With passion in his voice, Nate said loud and clear, "Your Honor, I beg you spare this man from a life in prison."

There was complete silence in the courtroom. Nate sat back down.

Judge Albright stared at Nate. After a moment, she asked if Terri Jo wished to make a statement.

Terri Jo nodded. She looked stunning as she

walked to the witness stand. She wore a peach-colored skirt with a pale blue blouse and matching earrings.

Terri Jo asked permission to be seated.

"Your Honor, I'm a student at the University of Northern Colorado on an art scholarship. I also attend art school at the Bemis School of Art in Colorado Springs in the summertime. All my life I've had a dream that I would someday be able to study art. I used to paint or sketch portraits of people when I was a child. My mother often posed for me while I drew pencil sketches of her."

Terri Jo explained how her mother and father were taken away from her and Nate. She tried using watercolors to paint her feelings on paper.

When Terri Jo said that, Nate noticed Jennings close his eyes. He pressed his hands to his face and looked at the floor.

"Many times I drew what I believed portrayed the accident scene in Shilshole Bay. You see, school counselors attempted to assist me through my grief when my parents were killed. They also suggested I try to visualize the face of the person or people who rammed my father's boat. But when I first saw the face of Tim Ford, I realized he in no way resembled the portrait I had in my mind. This may seem odd, Your Honor, but today has turned my life around. I find myself reunited with a brother I presumed lost to me forever. I found my dad's partner and the man who babysat me a few times, Detective Jennings. And you know, now I know who was responsible for killing my mom and dad."

Terri Jo reached for a tissue from the box beside the witness stand. Then she continued. "As I went to bed last night, I asked myself, how would society benefit by my saying that Mr. Ford should be sent to prison? Would I prevent his children from pursuing their dreams because their father was away in prison? Your Honor, I ask you not to imprison Mr. Ford. I'm afraid I'll always see his face and picture him in a jail cell if he's sent to prison. I can't imagine painting a portrait of Mr. Ford under those conditions."

Terri Jo looked right at Judge Albright. Her hands were shaking. Then she got up and joined her brother.

Judge Albright appeared moved by Terri Jo's words. She remained silent for a few moments. Then she made some notes before she looked up at those in the courtroom.

"I believe there is one more person to return to the speaker's stand. Am I correct, Mrs. Ford?"

Melissa Ford looked pale as she walked from her seat in the front of the courtroom.

Once again, Judge Albright invited her to be seated in the witness chair. She wrung her hands as she looked toward her husband. She began to speak.

"Oh, God," she said. "What will I do without

you, Tim? Judge, what can I say? My husband isn't a bad person. You've got to see that. He doesn't drink or gamble, not even smoke. I couldn't want a better man. He's paid for his mistake. He's paid over and over again. We've all paid for his carelessness so many times. And we'll continue to pay. What good can come of his going to prison? I'm not afraid of going to work. I'm really not afraid of that. I fear for my two children. They are already paying a price being taunted by other kids. You've got to see, Your Honor, to understand our plight." She broke down crying.

"This hearing stands adjourned until tomorrow at ten when I'll pronounce the sentence."

Leaving the courtroom, Nate, Terri Jo, Misty, and Jennings remained silent until they got off the elevator on the first floor.

Misty suggested Terri Jo cancel her hotel reservations for the night and stay with her and Nate. Terri Jo thanked her, but she wanted to stay in her hotel room.

Jennings suggested they freshen up and meet for dinner. Nate and Misty headed to their car. Ted gave Terri Jo a lift to her hotel.

At dinner, Jennings brought up the penalty phase of Ford's case. He was positive the judge would hand out a stiff sentence. Jennings thought Ford would get ten to twenty years with the possibility of early parole for good behavior.

"I know I'm looking at this in a different way, I guess, since us cops see crime all the time. I loathe criminals. Ford may not exactly fit the mold of repeat offenders, really tough creeps. I kinda see him as the three of you do, but like I say, I'm a cop, and my job is catching crooks and seeing them off the streets. I feel for their families, for Ford's family too. I guess you catch my drift."

Misty said, "I'm trying to figure out what the judge will do. I guess we'll just have to wait till tomorrow. But I'm so glad Nate and Terri Jo found each other."

With a burst of enthusiasm, Jennings said, "Let's drink a toast to the reunion, oops, well ... "

"That's fine. Nate'll have a soft drink. Okay, honey?"

Terri Jo looked a bit puzzled. "Is there something wrong, Nate? Are you all right?"

Nate looked at his sister. "We've been so interested in you, Terri Jo, we haven't gotten around to telling much of what I've done, or maybe undone."

Terri Jo said, "You sure look like you could take on the world, Nate."

Jennings interrupted, "Well, let's have a toast. Let me call a waitress over."

"If I were gonna tell my life's history," Nate said, "it would include some nightmares, Terri Jo. I had a drinking problem. I mean, a serious drinking problem. I was a bum, a drifter."

"What! Oh my God," Terri Jo said. "But you look great, so healthy. Doesn't he, Misty?"

"I only knew Nate for his healthy side. And the longer I knew him, the healthier he became, other than getting hurt in the ring."

"What ring? What does that mean, Nate?"

"Like I said, I haven't told you everything yet. I was a prizefighter, a good one. I retired without one loss, except I got hurt in my last fight. It's a long story, Terri Jo. But that's all over now. A number of people helped me, and if I were to tell you something about Tim Ford, you'd never believe that either."

"About what? What about him? What does that have to do with your life other than his almost destroying ours from what you say?"

"I found a dollar bill on the street in Las Vegas."

"Las Vegas? What were you doing in Las Vegas?"

"Like I said, I was drinking wine, lots of it. I stumbled on to a dollar bill that may have been tossed out the door of a tour bus. I know it sounds crazy, but Ted told me that Ford threw a dollar bill out the door of a tour bus. I think that's the dollar I picked up. Things changed from that moment on."

"So," Jennings said. "That's why you've been asking about that dollar bill thing, Nate?"

They toasted their happiness, although it was somewhat dimmed by Tim Ford's impending sentencing.

Jennings said, "Good night. I'll leave the three of you to fill in all the blanks." Nate, Misty, and Terri Jo went to Terri Jo's hotel room, where they spent the rest of the evening getting caught up.

At midnight, Nate and Misty left for their hotel.

• • •

Judge Albright entered the courtroom with papers in her hand and called the court to order. She asked if anyone else wished to speak before she passed sentence. No one responded.

She reached for her notes and said, "Mr. Ford, please rise."

Ford and his lawyer stood.

"Mr. Ford, you entered a plea of guilty as to manslaughter in the first degree. In response to that plea, the penalty is ten to twenty years in a state prison. However, I'm responding to the statements made on your behalf. They were powerful." She paused for a moment, looking directly at Tim Ford. "I can't ignore the statements made by Johnny Bradford's fellow police officers. They asked me to be severe in handing out punishment. I have searched for a compromise, one that hopefully will satisfy all parties concerned."

Nate became aware of what was happening among the people in the courtroom, like a movie camera had appeared to take close-ups of the scene.

Melissa Ford bowed her head. Detectives Carron, Forrestor, and Jennings's eyes appeared to be riveted on the judge. The Bradfords, along with Misty, also stared at the judge. Misty dabbed at tears welling up in her eyes. Nate knew she was trying to maintain her composure, and he loved her for that.

The judge continued. "I've contacted Mr. Ford's employers and secured a proposition from them as follows. Mr. Ford will be allowed to work five days a week within the confines of his employer's office building. He may return home on weekday evenings and nights. He will not be allowed out of that building at any time during his work hours. He will be confined to jail in the County Criminal Justice Center on weekends and legal holidays for a period of five years. After five years, if Mr. Ford has complied without default, he shall be allowed to return to his regular position as a salesperson. In his sales capacity at that time, he will be allowed away from the physical confines of his workplace.

"In addition to the five years of weekend confinement, I will order Mr. Ford to render to this county five more years of community service such as speaking before youth groups about the hazards of alcohol use. He'll also conduct classes on watercraft safety. The community service events must be held at least once a month."

The judge thumbed through some of her notes and said, "I'm assigning an officer of the court to this case. He will present evidence to the court of Mr. Ford's compliance with this sentence for the first five years and then for the following five years. I will give out the total details of this sentencing procedure to Mr. Ford's defense attorney and to the prosecuting attorney. I order that Mr. Ford remain in custody until tomorrow when he shall report to work. I repeat: he will return to jail every weekend and holiday following this hearing. This sentence begins tomorrow."

Judge Albright tapped her gavel. "The court is adjourned."

Nate, Misty, Terri Jo, and Jennings simply sat expressionless. Detectives Carron and Forrestor looked at each other as if in dismay.

Melissa Ford ran to her husband and hugged him.

Just as the bailiffs began to escort Tim Ford out of the courtroom, Ford looked at Detective Ted Jennings and the Bradfords and said, "I thought I would never be able to look at you people. I still don't seem to be worthy, but thank you so much. I hope someday you'll be able to totally forgive me."

Nate looked at him without smiling, but Misty spoke up and said, "Maybe someday they will. Maybe."

Reporters crowded around the steps of the courthouse as Nate and Terri Jo appeared, shouting

JOEY CHISESI AND DIANE CHISESI

questions at them, shoving microphones in their faces.

Jennings ran interference as they pushed their way through the throng. "Knock it off. Let them be. Can't you see they've been through enough? Out of our way, please. Come on now. Move. They have nothing to say to you."

One television reporter challenged Jennings to answer what he thought his fellow police officers would think about the leniency Ford received. "My police brothers understand. They're human beings, not robots. But I'm sure they're disappointed."

Jennings pleaded with them again, saying, "Look, just back off with your questions. We'll issue a statement later. I promise you."

Nate suggested they cross the street to The Justice for something to drink. A few reporters chased after them, but no one responded to the reporters. Soon the wolf pack of reporters stopped their pursuit.

Once seated, Jennings said, "I'm afraid I'm not going to keep my promise to be interviewed. The local media'll chase me down at precinct headquarters, but I'm gonna put them off as long as I can. Meanwhile, you guys can be on your way home."

Misty pleaded with Terri Jo to change her train ticket and come back to the winery with them. After some cajoling, Terri Jo agreed.

Nate said, "Terri Jo, you can stay with us as long

• • •  248  • • •

as you want. How soon do you have to be back at school?"

"Oh, I can miss a week. They'll understand. We don't receive grades for assignments and exams. Instead the school teaches us techniques to use in our artwork. I really like the Bemis program. Of course, I like my university studies too. They're both great."

After a light snack, Jennings said his good-byes to the three of them, promising to pay a visit to the winery in the near future. "You know, the past few days have been filled with stress and sadness for all of us, but the good side is getting to see you Bradford kids grown up. You're very special people. And now, I've gotten to know another special lady. Misty, the guy you've chosen is quite a man. I can't say enough about Nate. I tell you, he sure picked a beautiful gal. Well, I'll leave you three now, and I promise you, someday I'll surprise you and be down to munch some cheese and sip some wine."

Jennings shook hands with everyone, almost losing his detective like composure as he did. "I love you, kids. So long for now." Jennings left the restaurant by a side door.

While Nate, Misty, and Terri Jo ordered dessert with their coffee, Terri Jo called AMTRAK and changed her reservation. They managed to avoid any lingering reporters as they left the restaurant.

The following morning, Nate and Misty took

Terri Jo to the AMTRAK station. She changed her ticket so she could stop in Roseville on her way back to Colorado.

Nate and Misty caught their flight to Sacramento a couple hours later. Byron met them at the Sacramento airport.

Nate drove Byron's car home. On the way, they brought Byron up to date on the court happenings. Byron nodded in approval. "I figured you'd be fair in your judgment of the guy. What I couldn't figure was the sentence the judge would dish up. Do you guys feel okay about it?"

Nate said, "Yes. I know it's still tough on his wife and kids, but you know, it could've been tougher. Yeah, I feel okay about it. I know my sister, Terri Jo, is in agreement with me." Misty nodded her head.

Misty said, "Oh Dad, you're going to love Nate's sister, Terri Jo. Wait till you meet her. She's an artist. And, Dad, she's beautiful. Someone should paint a portrait of her."

"Well, from what you told me about her on the phone, she'll sure be a welcome guest. Yes, sir," Byron said. "Gosh, two beautiful ladies in my home at the same time. My blood pressure will probably go up again."

Nate and Misty picked up Terri Jo at the AMTRAK depot later the next day.

During her visit, Nate filled Terri Jo in on his messed-up life prior to meeting Misty. While listening to Nate's previous nightmarish life, Terri Jo cried. Nate felt good when she put her head on his shoulder. As he talked, he realized how much he'd missed his love for his sister all these years.

A few days later, it was time for Terri Jo to leave the winery, but not before Nate and Misty made a pledge with her to visit each other at least once a year. Her departure back to Greeley and UNC was filled with both joy and sadness.

# EPILOGUE

"How could we be happier?" That was the question Misty often asked Nate. He and Misty were now a family that included twins—Keith Byron, a boy, and Kalen Rose, a girl. Rose was Misty's mother's name while Keith's middle name was Misty's dad's. At one time, the couple had considered naming the twins after Nate's parents. They decided against that. They thought it better not to have constant reminder of Nate's loss of his parents when he was a youngster.

When the twins were three, something unexpected happened. Nate was readying the winery for a formal dinner for a group when Misty called Nate on the intercom. "Nate," she said. "Please come home as soon as possible." Nate's heart began to pound. He jumped into the jeep and skid to a halt in the driveway. A fancy new BMW sat parked there.

He found Byron and Misty seated at the kitchen table. With them sat a well-dressed man. The twins sat on the floor playing with their toys.

"Oh, Nate," Misty said, "I'd like you to meet Charles Brubaker. Mr. Brubaker represents the Hein and Hoth Development Company. They're located in Roseville."

Brubaker stood and extended a hand of greeting to Nate. Byron urged Nate to sit down at the table with them. There was a glass of Nate's favorite raspberry iced tea waiting for him, along with a glass of the same tea in front of the others. Brubaker sat back down and said, "Nate, may I call you that?"

"Yes, of course," Nate said.

"Nate, I'm here to make Byron an offer I believe you'll be pleased to hear. I've already spoken to him and your wife, but I'll repeat it to you. I've been retained by Hein and Hoth to acquire the Wakefield Vineyard and Winery for them…but not as an ongoing winery operation."

"I'm not sure I understand what you mean, Mr. Brubaker."

"Call me Chuck."

"Oh, sure. Thanks. Okay, Chuck, what does as an operational winery mean?"

"Well, I suppose it means Hein and Hoth would like to purchase the winery and vineyard, if you will. Own the land. They're developers and builders. I'm sure they'll no doubt level the winery. Their plans are to build luxury homes on this site, expensive homes, really expensive homes."

"Oh," Nate said, not too surprised at the statement.

"Right then," Byron said. "You and I've talked about the possibility that this would happen some-day, Nate. I guess this may be the first day of our future lives."

Brubaker said, "The future's the present. It's right now, folks. I must tell you this is an opportunity not to be missed. We, Hein and Hoth, that is, know of the fabulous reputation you've earned with Wakefield Wines. We know of your business acumen. We pretty well know the total picture involving the winery, its special events, the vineyard, and I suspect your personal attachment to the whole scenario except, of course, your annual income. That part of the equation's not my job."

Nate and Misty sat silent as Byron questioned Brubaker.

"You've left out this beautiful house. It's been my home for twenty-five years. That would be the toughest thing for me to let go. Then to think of its bein' taken down to the ground. That's a mighty big pill to swallow, don't you think?"

"Good point," said Brubaker. "In fact, an excellent point. My clients have a very respectable offer concerning your home. It is beautiful, and the landscaping is gorgeous. It would fit right into the developer's plans for this acreage. I suppose I shouldn't disclose the five potential owners of the estate homes to be built, but we don't have any reason to withhold that information. In other words, we considered your feelings about your estate and grounds, to be specific. Here's what we're prepared to extend to you."

Brubaker reached into his briefcase and pulled out a group of papers. "We've been to the Placer County recorder's office and examined the tract of land Hein and Hoth hope to acquire. Oh, by the way, we studied other land areas here also. Your two hundred acres became our first priority, however. But getting back to your house proper. We feel your house would blend into our overall scheme of things. It would be an asset to the building project. We don't see this house presenting any objection to prospective home buyers. They'll come from an extremely wealthy background. I'm sure you're aware that two Hollywood stars already own big homes in your county. Am I right?"

Byron nodded. "I've known that for some time. Don't tell me the rich folks down south want out of the LA area? Or do they think there's gold in our hills?"

"You know, Byron, there's gold here all right, but it's in a different form." Brubaker cleared his throat. "As to gold, real gold in the ground, I don't need to tell you that gold was mined just a few miles south and east of here. Am I correct?"

"Yep," said Byron, "I've often wondered if any of the tailin's reached here. I never dug deep enough to find out though. Never panned in the streams here either."

"Let me tell you this," Brubaker went on. "Hein and Hoth won't build any homes here on speculation. They'll all be custom designed on some thirty-five-acre parcels, ordered and paid for by TV and film people. And they'll be lived in. As we see it, these rich people are tired of breathing foul air, seeing forest fires all around them, and worrying about crime statistics."

"But you were going to mention my dad's home," Misty spoke up. "What were you saying about this house?"

"We'll agree to let your home remain. We would give you a lease for one hundred years at one dollar a year with a renewable option at the end of the one hundred years on the same terms. In other words, Byron, a perpetual lease for as long as you, or anyone else in your family should choose to live here. I can't think of a land deal that would be more appealing to anyone. Right?"

Nate felt taken back by the proposal. He wasn't

sure he understood everything Brubaker had just said.

Byron looked at Nate and Misty. "That sounds all well and good, but how would we ever adjust to never seein' the winery itself and those rows of grapes ... my gold?"

A hundred-year lease? Nate knew Byron wasn't going to live for another hundred years. Neither would he and Misty.

"Thought of that too, Byron. We'll leave you ten acres of land to grow grapes, your very own gold. If I may be so rash as to say, I think you'll watch your money grow instead of grapes. Here's Hein and Hoth's offer. They'll pay you thirty million dollars for your land and house. That, people, is a lot of grapes ... a lot of gold!"

Nate couldn't believe what he'd just heard. He looked at Misty and her dad. They stared at each other in amazement.

Brubaker said, "Those cute children of yours should have their college monies pretty well guaranteed, wouldn't you say?"

"Sounds like the entertainment world has money they haven't found yet," Nate said. "Sure you're not going to build another Disneyland down here or a Knott's Berry Farm North? If so, will they be looking for a manager?"

That made everyone laugh. "I'm not only sure; we've put the offer in writing. I've also been to the

Placer County Planning Commission. They have mixed emotions over this, just as I'm sure you do. But that's our risk. We wouldn't be venturing into this situation if we thought the builder's proposal would fall through."

Silence filled the room. Then, to Nate's surprise, Byron said, "You know, I think the offer's quite fair, but this is somethin' the three of us need to discuss. There's no way I can give you an answer today."

"That's good enough, folks. I didn't expect you to leap without thought. I do need to be somewhat hard-nosed, however. After all, that's my job. This offer is only good for sixty days. My people won't raise the ante, I assure you of that. Personally, I think it's a very decent proposal, more than fair."

Brubaker laid papers on the table, saying, "Here's the offer in writing, everything I spoke of. I'm sure you have an attorney. Why not show this to your legal eagle?" Brubaker smiled. "You might consider this akin to winning the lottery."

With that he stood and reached out to shake hands with each of them. He thanked them for their time and headed to the door.

Misty waited for a break in Nate and Byron's conversation and then said, "You know, Dad, a few years ago when you had the stroke, I prayed for something like this to happen. You know how terribly concerned we were over your health back then. But you're as good as new."

"Hey, I'm in my fifties. That's new?"

"Well, almost new," Nate said. "Just kiddin', guys."

"If this offer is as he said it is, and I have no reason to doubt it, you two would never again have to worry about grape crop failure, the weather, insects, the price of wine, getting a crew to work here, all of those things," Byron said.

Nate began to pace. "They just might be those things that keep people going. I saw a discussion on TV about good and bad stress. Good stress is just that, good for you. The bad stress is the killer. Right, By?"

Misty jumped right in. "This has been your life, Dad. There wouldn't be anything to look forward to, except, well, fun types of things."

"You mean like golf and fishin'," Byron said. "I can take golf lessons. Always wanted to play that darn game. Just never had time for it before. I understand you're never too old to learn golf."

Byron picked up the papers left by Brubaker. He said, "Nate, mind photocopyin' these? Let's see if we can figure out what he really said. Why don't we relax and think about what this means to each of us, kinda like a combination of thinkin' and carin' about one another. Okay? Each of us gets a copy of the offer. This meetin' stands adjourned."

Two days went by. Byron and Nate were setting up tables and chairs for a luncheon at the winery when Byron asked Nate if he'd like more time to think about the offer. Nate said, "No. But I think you and Misty and I should talk now." Byron got one of the workers to come finish what he'd been doing. Nate did the same. They drove up to the house to find Misty.

"Want some milk, fellows? I have chocolate chip cookies. Wait, what are you both doing here in the middle of the day? Everything okay?"

"What? Spoil our lunch? Ruin our figures?" Nate laughed.

"Just some of that great raspberry tea will do fine," Byron said. "We all need to get energized!"

Misty poured the tea, and the three sat down at the table.

"Where are the kids?" Nate asked.

"Oh, they went for a walk," Misty said. "They're exploring for gold with the babysitter."

"Don't tell me they can read maps already," piped in Nate.

"How's that?" Byron chuckled. "Did the kids find the gold in the offer Brubaker left?"

Misty laughed.

Byron then started the conversation again. "I've been tossin' this offer around. I like it. I know you're concerned over my welfare. I'm glad. That's as it should be. Nate, you're the son I never had, and Misty, I love you like no one in the world.

"Me too," Nate said.

"My thinkin' goes this way," Byron said. "I'll split the thirty million with you. That's fifteen million for me and the same for you two. We'll be able to live here and not have to leave our home. We'll just have the expense of runnin' a household and a small vineyard. As I see this offer, those guys will have to pay the taxes since they'll be leasin' the property to us for a buck a year. What more could we ask? I've decided the word *retire* sounds pretty good."

Nate saw Misty's eyes cloud over.

Byron continued. "Misty, when my grandkids are old enough to go to preschool, something like that, you might just want to land a position with the library system out here. That is, if you want a job. Or maybe just stay home with the kids."

Misty nodded.

"And, Nate, with your experience the last four years, you're certain to find a position in management, maybe finish up gettin' your college education."

Nate stared at the table. He wasn't sure what Byron was getting at.

"Excuse me for plannin' both of your futures. Heck, you might wind up with seven kids or so. Then we'd have to add on to this house."

Nate spoke first. "By, it's not our place to determine what you do. Mist and I figure this is your decision to make, not ours. We stand by anything you decide. You've been something special to me.

You know that. And Misty, well, Mist would go to hell and back for you. You should pardon the expression."

Byron reached across the table and took one of Misty's and Nate's hands. "I've already made an appointment with Mitchell Sorenson. Mitch has been handling my legal affairs for years now. He's sharp and he's honest. We're to see him tomorrow. Get your babysitter so you can come along if you'd like."

The next day, the babysitter arrived to watch over the twins. Then the three drove to attorney Sorenson's office in Roseville. He examined the purchase offer and found no legal problems.

"Congratulations, Byron. Seems like you folks may have just won the lottery. Hein and Hoth are well-known land developers. According to the contract, the entire burden is on them. All you need to do is accept the terms. I'll draw an acceptance agreement and get it to their representative, Brubaker, after you sign it, Byron. I'll ask them to deposit the funds in an escrow account we'll set up."

"What papers do I need to get hold of, Mitch?" Byron said.

"You'll need your title papers and a survey of the vineyard and winery with your house located on it. In the meantime, the title company will do a title search ensuring Hein and Hoth that the land is clear. I know you haven't made a loan against your property, so that will be cut and dry. The recorder's office will document the transaction. I'll recommend a title company, and they'll provide Hein and Hoth with a new title and deed in their name."

Misty said, "You're sure Dad's house will remain and the extra land this man Brubaker promised dad will all be included?"

"Yes, that's all in the offer. They have to adhere to it. If not, no deal."

Nate, viewing all of this, had not said a word. He wondered if he should express his thoughts.

Then he spoke up. "By, are you absolutely certain this is what you want?"

"For sure, Nate. I'm positive. What I'm doin' is the best for all of us. If I hadn't had that doggone little stroke, I might be hesitatin'. But I'm convinced this is the way to go."

Sorenson added, "Your dad is going to have to change his will, and we're going to use a trust agreement, what with all this money coming into his estate. In fact, you folks can either go in the waiting room or, if it's okay with Byron, just sit here while I get some details from him."

"Hey, they're my life, Mitch. They're everythin' to me. They can sit right here."

"Good," Sorenson said.

Misty and Nate became beneficiaries of Byron's new trust agreement. His attorney promised to have the papers in the mail to Byron in a few days.

"You need to check things over, Byron. Return the preliminary papers to me, and I'll have Margie put everything together for your final signature. We'll get them witnessed and have a notary sign them."

"Well, that should do it for now, except Misty and Nate. You two should create trusts too. I'm not supposed to represent beneficiaries at the same time I represent your dad, but in California I can do that by you folks signing a special form. I'll have Margie get you some literature about trusts if you wish. Give me a call when you're ready. How's that sound?"

"Oh, fine," replied Nate. "This is all so sudden. It's like I've been hit in the jaw by a right hook."

Misty said, "We don't talk about right or left hooks anymore, do we, Dad?"

"Nope…only if we're watchin' some other bruisers on the tube!"

Nate grinned. "I take back what I said."

"Here, Misty. Use my cell phone and call the sitter. Check on the kids and see if she'll be all right stayin' another couple hours or so. Let's go and have a really nice meal. I've worked up an appetite. We'll pretend Hein and Hoth are buyin'," Byron said.

"And they are, Dad," Misty added. "They really are."

. . .

That evening, Nate and Misty were in bed after tucking the three-year-olds in for the night. Misty turned her head toward Nate and whispered, "I can't believe the last three days, honey. Can you?"

Nate looked at his Misty, so happy, so beautiful.

Misty whispered, "To think we have a son and daughter and now we're close to fifteen million dollars."

Nate couldn't resist saying, "Mist, got change for a dollar?"